MW00939977

CUPID STUPID

RETURN TO CUPID, TEXAS

SYLVIA MCDANIEL

VIRTUAL BOOKSELLER

Nothing says bad judgement like trying to prove a superstition true...

Taylor Braxton, along with a few adventurous girlfriends, decide to test the Cupid superstition the day Taylor's ex-fiancé is to be married. A few bottles of wine help lower her inhibition and go a long way to giving her courage. After all, Taylor reasons, what is the worst thing that can happen – the superstition of finding her true love might come true?

Sheriff Ryan Jones is used to getting calls about the odd dancing around the downtown fountain. When you live in Cupid, Texas, there were always some residents who believed if you dance naked around the fountain, you were guaranteed to find your true love. What he doesn't expect is to find the lovely, but spirited Taylor Braxton confronting him at midnight – sans clothing.

Will the Cupid Superstition help Taylor and Ryan overcome the past and take a chance on love again? Or will a promise he made deflect Cupid's arrow?

Receive a free book when you sign up for my new book alerts!

To Krystal Shannan
For your dedication to helping authors and also Autism and helping us
all reach the USA TODAY Best Sellers List! THANK YOU!!

Southern Historical Romance
A Scarlet Bride

The Cuvier Women
Wronged
Betrayed
Beguiled
Boxed Set

Receive a free book when you sign up for my new book alerts!

❀ Created with Vellum

CHAPTER 1

*C*upid, Texas

"Valentine's Day. Today is the cheating snake's wedding day," Taylor Braxton said, flipping her blonde hair over her shoulder before taking a sip of wine. Her third glass of the evening. "I'd like to propose a toast to his new wife. May she never find him in her bed with someone else, like I found her in mine."

The three women clinked glasses.

"Maybe it was for the best. After all, lawmen are known for being serial cheaters," Meghan, one of Taylor's best friends, said in her quiet librarian voice. She gave a shake of auburn hair, her emerald eyes filled with sympathy.

Still the same after all these years, Taylor wondered if Meghan ever raised her voice even during a climax. Did she scream with passion, or just say oh? And Taylor never wanted to know the answer to that question.

Yes, lawmen cheated, but many men were sleaze bags who thought infidelity was nothing.

Kelsey, Taylor's other best friend leaned in close. "Well, if you hadn't found him locked in the arms of another woman, you wouldn't have come back to Cupid."

"True," Taylor agreed.

Pushing her dark brunette hair back over her shoulder, Kelsey smiled. "I can't believe we're all here together again. Just like the old days when we were young and naive and so vulnerable. Now, we're all grown up and--"

"Still single," Meghan said with a sigh.

"Yep, no eligible man on my radar," Kelsey admitted. "Who would want to date a woman with three pain in the ass brothers watching over her?"

Kelsey's announcement surprised Taylor. Of the three of them, Kelsey was who she thought would walk down the aisle first. Instead, not one of them was wearing a ring, and frankly, she found it odd she'd come the closest to a honeymoon.

"I don't want a man. I'm giving up. I'm going to remain single the rest of my life," Taylor announced.

After her last attempt at love, the time to step away had arrived in the form of a revealed booty call. Now, her focus on the family business was the most important thing in her life.

"Oh yeah, that's the life I want," Meghan replied, sarcasm dripping in her tone. "Always the third wheel when you're around couples. Every holiday your relatives asking if there is something wrong with you or have you tried online dating. Blind dates with your next-door neighbor's son, who is so kind that he still lives with his mother." She shivered. "No, thanks."

Meghan's appearance fitted the sweet, innocent librarian image, but her tongue was sharp and precise. Sometimes even Taylor was shocked at what came out of her smart mouth.

Setting her wine glass down on the table Kelsey leaned forward. "Or your brothers' glancing at every man you bring home like he's a terrorist, and should they learn he's sleeping with their sister, he would wake up six feet under." Kelsey giggled. "They don't know, but I lost my virginity the first semester of college during pledge week."

"Ohh...with someone you cared about?" Taylor asked.

She sighed. "Not really. We were two virgins who wanted to rid ourselves of the stigma. A fumbling, truly awful, awkward experience. After that horrible first time, I concentrated on my studies and not on men."

"What about you, Taylor? When did you lose your virginity?" Meghan asked.

"Prom night," she said, shaking her head. "Billy Ray Smith."

"Oh my gosh, he's married and living one town over."

"Thank God. He was mistake number one. I was young and foolish." And oh, so stupid, she thought.

That night he'd convinced her everyone was doing the nasty and if she didn't give it up, she would be the only virgin left in school. Curious about the forbidden fruit and wanting to fit in, she listened to him.

Meghan laughed. "Well, we certainly know who popped my cherry. Max Vandenberg, football superstar jerk."

The three women sighed. Kelsey shifted uneasily in her chair. "We thought we were going to change the world."

Taylor snickered. "I think the world changed us."

Meghan giggled. "Remember that silly superstition from high school?"

"Which one? There were several," Kelsey said. "I especially liked the one where the football boys had to put a pair of girl's panties on the top of the goal post if they wanted a winning season."

So many things happened in a small town where gridiron was king. The football team could get away with so much more than the other school sports.

"While the drill team practiced in our uniforms, all our undies were stolen from the girls' gym. I remember going commando, like, yesterday." Taylor chuckled.

Kelsey turned toward her. "Max Vandenberg was the panty thief. Did you hear that he played professional football for the Dallas Cowboys for a while?"

"Until he got hurt. Now he's back." Meghan shook her head. "Right back here under my nose - the big jerk. He's coaching at my school."

"Why does it seem like many of our classmates left and eventually returned."

"Yes, Ryan Jones is back. My brother told me he's sheriff now," Kelsey said, drinking another glass of vino. "He was my ex. So two exes back in town and another one's married and lives nearby."

"I don't consider Billy Ray an ex."

Sure, Taylor lost her virginity the night of prom, but recognized she would never marry Billy Ray. *Redneck* was a polite term for that kid. The ex that crushed her was in Dallas where he belonged with his skanky new wife.

Sitting there, she glanced at her besties from grade school.

"Wonder how many girls fell for that Cupid superstition? Did you guys ever do that one?" Taylor asked.

"Oh no," Meghan said. "I didn't like getting undressed in gym class."

"Oh no," Kelsey echoed. "If my brothers caught me dancing naked around the statue in the town square, I would have been sealed away in a nunnery until my female parts shriveled. What about you?"

"No," she said, thinking she didn't believe that nonsense.

Taylor looked at the two women sitting at the table. She poured the last of the second bottle of wine. The music seemed louder, the laughter shriller, and yet she was having so much fun, she didn't want to stop. Tomorrow she'd probably regret the amount of alcohol they were consuming, but tonight felt good. Old friends, memories, and alcohol helping her forget the importance of this damn day.

"You remember when all the cheerleaders did the naked Cupid dance, all hoping to find their true love. How did the magic work out for them?" Kelsey said with a laugh.

Taylor shook her head. "I remember. The football team showed up unexpectedly with cameras in hand and when the squad returned to school they faced suspension."

The principal had decided to make them examples.

Meghan frowned and gazed at the women, her blue eyes large, her expression one of disgust. "Don't feel too badly for them. They're all married. In fact, most of them have babies. If the superstition is true, it worked very well for them. What the hell is wrong with us?"

Taylor threw her hands up. "I'm not looking to get married. Right now, my focus is my parents' restaurant. I don't need a man."

After her disastrous engagement, the time had come to put the idea of marriage and children and happily ever after on the shelf.

Turning in her chair, Meghan looked at Kelsey. "What about you? Do you want to marry?"

Kelsey leaned on her hands. "Yes, I would like to find a man, but my brothers run them off faster than a deer during hunting season. So I'll be working on the boutique I'm preparing to open for business. One year is all I have to make a profit. Or I'll be moving back to the city. What about you, Meghan?"

She tossed back her hair and stared them straight in the eye. "I'm twenty-five years old. I'm ready. My ovaries are beginning to shrivel like a prune. Bring on the right man and I'll race him to the altar."

The idea hit Taylor smack in the stomach, and while it seemed preposterous, the idea was too good to pass up. She shook her head at the two of them, giggling. "Then let's do it."

Frowns appeared on their faces as they stared at her. "What?"

She checked her watch. "It worked for all those other women.

5

Why not us? The superstition says at midnight anyone chanting and dancing naked around the fountain will soon meet their true love. I've never believed in the notion, but hey, I'm game. We've got thirty minutes. Let's go kick some Cupid butt and see if that superstition is real or not."

Meghan's eyes widened. "You want me to take off my clothes and dance in front of you and everyone else in town, chanting some silly verse?"

"Oh, most people will be asleep and I've seen you *au naturel* before. I'll be too busy dancing to notice you and your jiggling tatas."

Laughing, Kelsey gazed at Taylor. "And you think this is going to work."

No, she didn't believe in superstitions. She walked under ladders, stepped on cracks, and black cats didn't frighten her. Friday the thirteenth was just another day and dancing without clothes around a statue wasn't going to land her a husband.

She didn't want or need a man in her life. But she'd do this for her friends.

"We're late bloomers. Everyone else did this in high school. We never had the courage, but now we're older, some of us desperate. Let's do it."

Kelsey lifted her glass and drained the alcohol. "I'm in. What about you, Meghan?"

"Oh, it's starting again. During high school, you girls could get me into more trouble. You're back in town less than twenty-four hours and already you're plotting mischief."

"Oh, come on, it'll be fun," Taylor said, downing the last of her drink and signaling the waitress.

"The temperature outside is colder than a well digger...and we're getting naked," Meghan whined. "Tonight, other women are being wined and dined and we're going to dance without our clothes, in the town square? Something is wrong with this picture."

"Think of the thrill. The tales you can tell your children," Taylor said, the adventure of doing something dangerous sending a ripple of excitement through her. Years had passed since her last prank and this was the kind of stunt that got her juices flowing.

"Daring." Kelsey grabbed her purse. "I haven't done anything like this since college. I'm just drunk enough my logical, rational side is being held hostage by my fun side."

"Are you in?" Taylor asked not certain Meghan would agree.

With a sigh Meghan finished her wine. "I don't want to be the only old maid. Of course, I'm in."

&

TAYLOR WAS GIGGLING HARD when they left the bar, the three of them laughing as they all but dragged poor Meghan. The girl was always a laggard, but give her enough alcohol and she knew how to party with the best of them. At least, she had years ago. They hadn't been bad kids, just teenagers testing their new adult skills and failing more often than not.

"I could be fired if we're caught," Meghan said. "Public nudity is not exactly the proper behavior for the school librarian. My contract says something about a moral issue."

Moral, schmoral - they weren't holding an orgy. A little silly fun that had gotten many kids in trouble.

Kelsey handed her the bottle of wine they'd managed to sneak out of the bar. "Take a swig, Meghan, it will give your courage a boost. Besides, we're not going to get caught. We're not stupid teenagers."

"No, we're stupid adults," Taylor said smiling. College was the last time she'd done anything this wild and crazy. Her sorority had broken into Phi Beta Kappa's house and stolen all the jock straps, greased them with Vaseline, and hung the undergarments in the trees outside the gym.

7

Clouds drifted across the moon casting eerie shadows and she felt a rush of excitement. "Five minutes until midnight. Hurry, girls."

Squealing, they ran the final two blocks to the fountain. They arrived, huffing and puffing, and stopped to stare at the sculptured God of Love.

"Dancing around this statue is going to help us find the man of our dreams?" Kelsey questioned. "Whoever made up this shit is sitting back somewhere laughing at how many fools stripped off their clothes and danced in the moonlight."

"In the middle of freaking winter," Meghan added.

Part of Taylor agreed with Kelsey, but the other part, the more reckless and wild part, urged her on. "Come on, girls, we're doing this. We're going to prove this is either the biggest farce in town, or it's going to work for my friends. Just not for me."

"I hope this is worth it," Meghan said as they all began to remove clothing, each one looking to make certain they weren't the only one stripping.

"Will it look funny if I leave my boots on?" Kelsey asked.

"Naked. You have to be naked according to the superstition," Taylor said, yanking off her footwear, the cold stones hard against her feet.

"As soon as the church bell strikes midnight, we're going to dance around the statue for one minute. Then I'm putting my clothes on and walking home," Meghan said, shivering in the buff. "You girls are going to be the death of me yet. If I come down sick--"

"We'll have a hot looking guy deliver you a box of Kleenex and chicken soup."

Kelsey started laughing. "Look, girls, I got a boob job while I was in college. Aren't they nice?"

She held up her tits for all to see and Meghan turned away groaning. "What am I doing?"

"I'm not looking at your breasts," Taylor said, giggling as she

8

removed her bra. Maybe this wasn't one of her smarter ideas. The cold had her own poor nipples shriveled to the size of a raisin.

"Hurry, midnight is almost here," Meghan said, her words slurred from the alcohol. "Let's do this and put our clothes back on before we catch pneumonia."

"We better get some action from this," Kelsey replied, jumping up and down on the sidewalk, nude.

"And not legal action," Taylor said with a giggle.

After she finished undressing, she folded her jeans and sweater neatly and placed them on a bench. "Okay, I'm ready. Let's do this."

Passing the bottle of wine one more time, laughing and chuckling and hoping the alcohol would give them some much needed warmth, Taylor tried not to look down.

"We're being so naughty," Meghan said, giggling drunkenly. "Never again."

"Oh, come on, next week we're taking you skinny dipping at the lake," Kelsey said.

"Not during the winter, we're not," Taylor replied.

The church bells started to chime. With a scream, they laughed and began to run and dance, giggling hysterically as the three of them ran around the God of love.

"Oh, Cupid statue find us our true love," they chanted as they danced nude around the fountain in the town square, laughing at the absurdness of what they were doing.

"Nuts," Meghan said. "All this is going to do is give us frostbite on our girly bits."

Taylor thought she might be right, but what a way to go. It felt freeing and exhilarating and she couldn't think of a single crazy thing that could pique this outing.

Headlights turned onto the street and they glanced at each other, their eyes wide. Shrieking, their hands trying to cover their female parts, they ran but their clothes were too far away.

SYLVIA MCDANIEL

"Oh no," Meghan said.

Red beacons flashed on top of the car. A shiver of fear raced down Taylor's spine setting panic into motion.

"Run, girls," Taylor yelled. "Run, it's the sheriff. Everyone split up, he can't arrest us all."

Kelsey and Meghan ran in different directions, running down the intersecting streets, leaving their clothes and purses behind.

Taylor wasn't departing without her boots. The footwear had set her back almost a month's pay and she couldn't leave them on a park bench. Grabbing her stuff, she tried to pick up her friends' as well, but her arms were full.

Lights shined on her.

"Halt," a man's voice instructed. "Drop everything."

Oh great, she was the one who would be going to jail for dancing in her birthday suit in the public square.

***

DURING FOOTBALL SEASON, Sheriff Ryan Jones caught one or two young teenage girls either about to dance or dancing naked around the Cupid statue. He kept encouraging the council to remove the statue, but tonight, three grown women with well developed female bodies were doing the Cupid Stupid move. Long legs, perfect round asses, and breasts that were mouthwatering tempting.

Sworn to protect and serve, he pushed the images from his brain and told his cock to go back to sleep. False emergency.

Valentine's Day, he'd meant to be here earlier before the bells dinged midnight, but the Raffsberger's cat created a disturbance in the alley that sent him on a feline pursuit. That pussy caused him more trouble than even the town drunk, Simon Connally. At least he could lock up Simon, but the feline stared at him with those laughing green eyes. Once again, the sheriff was on a cat chase.

Missing midnight, he'd arrived just in time to find three nude women dancing and chanting around the God of Love. And one of them was none other than Taylor Braxton. A girl from high school who if he hadn't been dating her best friend, he would have chased. But that was years ago.

"Don't move," he yelled, jumping out of his car and walking toward her. He didn't pull out his gun, because frankly, he didn't think she qualified as a dangerous criminal.

"Hi, Sheriff," she said, chattering and shivering in the cold, her arms crossed over her breasts, a palm covering her womanly bits. "How are you tonight?"

"I'm warmer than you," he replied, unable to stop his eyes from taking advantage of her nakedness. "Aren't you a little old for this?"

Jumping up and down, her arms wrapped across her breasts as she tried to get warm, he admired her curves. Since he'd been her best-friend's boyfriend right up until graduation, he never had a chance to pursue Taylor before leaving for the military. And it was just as well given how Kelsey let everyone know her feelings about him when they broke up.

"Desperate times call for desperate measures," Taylor said, her teeth clicking as she shivered.

"Oh, you're desperate to find love?" Maybe it was his lucky night after all.

"No, but my friends think they're sitting on the shelf. I don't need a man."

Oh crap, he didn't like the sound of this conversation, and during his time in the Marines, those words were repeated to him more times than he cared to admit.

He laughed. "One of those."

"What do you mean one of those?" she asked, her voice rising. "Don't you think you could let me put my clothes on?"

He ignored her statement. One of the consequences of her Cupid Stupid dance was what he called his law enforcement embarrassment. Sometimes in order to keep people from doing a silly thing more than once, you let them experience the effects of their actions. "A woman who is anti-men."

She shrugged. "Maybe. Maybe I have reason to be."

Walking behind her, he took out his cuffs. "Place your hands behind your back."

"Oh, come on, Ryan, you know I'm not dangerous."

Sure, he knew she wasn't threatening, but she needed to be taught a scary lesson.

"You're breaking the law," he said, leaning in close. A whiff of her breath let him know she'd consumed alcohol. "I'd say you're intoxicated and naked and both of those are against the law."

"We had a little too much fun."

"Come on, uncross your arms and put them behind your back," he said, feeling like he was being mean, but making an example of her so her girlfriends wouldn't be tempted to try again.

Moving her arms to the back, he almost regretted her compliance. She had a nice set of breasts that made his job even more difficult.

"Your girlfriends ran off and left you to face the consequences of your actions," he responded, slipping the cuffs around her wrists.

"Look, we were celebrating my ex getting married on Valentine's Day. We drank too much wine and decided we never did this in high school. We'd do it now."

A twinge of sympathy gripped his stomach. Okay, perhaps she had a reason to be drinking.

"I ruined the party," he said, glancing around the park, knowing they were long gone or just waiting for the opportunity to claim their clothes. "Where did your friends take off to? They're also under arrest."

"Oh no," Taylor said. "I'm not talking. I'm not giving up any information on them."

Strolling to the bench, he observed all the clothing. "They left their purses and clothes behind."

She cursed. Opening the first handbag, he pulled out the driver's license. "Meghan Scott. Isn't she the new school librarian? The school board will be displeased to hear she's got a warrant out."

He remembered the cute little auburn spitfire from school. She'd seemed so sweet and innocent and seeing her naked butt running down the street was quite pleasant.

"Please, Ryan, she didn't want to do this and I convinced her. She'll be fired."

"I can tell you who the third person is without even opening her purse. Kelsey Lawrence."

Taking the heap of clothing to his car, he grabbed a blanket from the backseat and carried it back to her. He didn't want to take her to jail. The paperwork, the embarrassment for her, the scarring of her permanent record. It was what he called the Stupid Cupid prank. Over the last two years, he'd seen it dozens of times.

Wrapping the woolen cloth around her, she lifted her chin defiantly and met his gaze. "You're really going to take me to jail?"

Not responding, he led her to his car and eased her into the back, like a common thief. She sighed, the sound dejected.

"I never thought I would have to call someone to bail me out."

"No, you never thought you would get caught dancing naked in the middle of town," he said, shutting the back door of his patrol car.

Crawling into the driver's seat he looked in the rearview mirror. "Where do you live?"

She frowned. "Nine twenty-six Hideaway Court. Why?"

He started the car and drove, letting her think he was taking her in. "Do you think your girlfriends are close by?"

"Don't have a clue. But you have their clothes. So I'm sure they're out of sight somewhere."

Chuckling, he drove to her townhouse only a couple blocks from downtown. "What did you do with your car?"

"I walked to the club. Due to the nature of our celebration, I thought it would be best to walk in case I had too much to drink. I didn't want to get a DUI or hurt someone."

Pulling in front of her house, she was quiet as he parked. Silence filled the automobile, even his radio had stopped crackling. Why did he feel like the boy in the diaper delivered him some good fortune? How did he go about asking a naked woman in the back seat of his patrol car for a date without looking like a real perv? He didn't.

"Every year, I arrest or take home kids who have decided to test the Cupid Stupid superstition. Seldom do I detain grownups, but if I do, I take them to the pokey where they belong. You're receiving a break for several reasons. One, you didn't drink and drive, and two, you said your ex was married today. For those two reasons, I'm giving you a pass. If I ever catch you near that damn sculpture, nude again, you will be charged and incarcerated."

Over the last year, he'd taken ten naked dumb kids home to their parents and only arrested one adult. And the reason the man had woken up incarcerated was because he'd been inebriated and waving his dick around peeing on the figure. City workers had to scrub the statue and drain the fountain while Ryan tried to convince the city council to knock down the God of Love.

"Thank you," she said, relief evident in her voice. "Are you going to press charges against my friends?"

"No, but you give them my warning. Any of you girls ever do this stunt again, I'll be waiting."

Usually his threat was enough to make people regret their decision.

"I'll remove the handcuffs and help you carry their stuff inside." He crawled out of the car.

Going to the back, he opened the door. "Lean forward."

As he unlocked the cuffs, his eyes feasted on her lovely rounded derrière.

"You know, I've never been cuffed before, and I must say they're very uncomfortable."

"They're supposed to be," he said and released her.

Pulling her arms in front of her she rubbed her wrists, keeping the blanket firmly tucked around her. Reaching for her hand, he helped her from the car. She stood and they were face to face, staring at each other, and he had the craziest urge to kiss her. Her lips were so ripe and full that he wanted to pluck them with his own. That craving would have to wait for another night.

"Thanks again, Ryan. I know what we did was crazy, but we didn't plan on getting caught."

"Nobody ever does. They think they're going to get away with the silly antic."

She stepped out of the way and he reached in and pulled out the stack of jeans, boots, and purses. "I'll drive around and see if I can find Meghan and Kelsey."

"They won't come out for you."

"It was nice of you to take the fall for them," he said, thinking not many women would do that for their friends.

"I persuaded them we should do this. I'm the one at fault."

"Yet, you don't want to marry?" he asked, shaking his head. "Seems kind of crazy."

"We did it for fun. Meghan wants to get married, but I barely escaped the noose once. I'm not looking for another chance," she said.

All he could think was, too bad. He'd been drawn to her in high school and now a mature woman, she was even better.

Hurrying to her door, she dug in her handbag for her key, the blanket sliding down, exposing her shoulder. Once the portal opened, a red dachshund greeted them, barking and yelping his

SYLVIA MCDANIEL

happiness at her being home, the dog's nails sticking in the blanket and edging it down.

"Zeus, down," she commanded.

Ryan followed behind her, carrying in the stack of clothes and boots. Boxes sat on the floor. The townhome had a homey atmosphere, but clearly she'd just moved back into town.

Turning to face him with the cloth tucked carefully around her hiding all her girly parts, she gazed at him. "Why don't you come by the restaurant one day and I'll fix something special for you. Not one of the regular items, but a specialty I'm working on not on the menu yet."

Now was not the time to ask her out; he knew dinner would be the perfect moment to ask.

"I'll come by tomorrow," he said.

"I'll have chicken picante waiting for you."

"Looking forward to it."

"Goodnight, Officer Ryan," she said and walked him to the door, shutting it behind him.

Stepping out onto the porch, he glanced up at the stars shining brightly. In Afghanistan, the nighttime stars had been brilliant, almost like he could reach out and touch them. A trickle of unease scurried down his spine and he pushed the memories away.

Maybe coming back to Cupid had been a good idea after all. Taylor Braxton had become a hot looking woman. All he had to do was convince her to go out with him. And he would, tomorrow.

CHAPTER 2

*T*he next morning at her family restaurant, the girls sat at a table, holding their heads in their hands. The morning crowd had slowed and Taylor sat with them nursing her own pounding head. "What were we thinking? By the way, I have your clothes and purses."

"Thank God," Kelsey said.

"I thought I would spend today on the phone cancelling credit cards. What a relief." Meghan glanced up, her blue eyes flashing with irritation. "We're lucky. Last night could have ended so badly. I could have lost my job. And now I'm beholding to the one jerk I never wanted to see again."

Grinning, Kelsey bent over and whispered, "Max really picked you up?"

"He saved my naked ass," she said, her voice a growl. "At first, I refused to climb into his car, but oh no, he insisted. Reminded me, if anyone else found me, I could kiss my career goodbye. What about you? Did you walk naked back to your place?"

Shaking her head, Kelsey glanced at her friends. "My brother's best friend Cody happened to be driving down the road. When his headlights flashed on me, I hid behind a skinny tree that didn't hide much."

"Oh dear. If your family finds out, your brothers will lock you up," Taylor responded.

"Cody promised me this would remain our secret, but I don't trust him. Men can't keep secrets," she said. "At any time, my phone will ring and my oldest brother will remind me of my obligations as a member of the Lawrence family."

Laughing, Meghan leaned back in the chair. "I can hear your brother reprimanding you so clearly. Does he always keep his nose in the stratosphere? He's a bigger snob than any woman."

"It's that whole family obligation. Keeping the name clear of any kind of scandal or disgrace. The very reason I stayed away from Cupid. The first time I act a little naughty, I get caught."

"Well, at least you made it home safely," Taylor said. She'd worried all night about her friends. "I was afraid to go searching for you and I couldn't call you as I had your cell phones."

"Yes, no thanks to you." Tossing her auburn hair over her shoulder, Meghan glared at Taylor.

"I'm sorry, Meghan. Until the sheriff arrived, we were having a good time."

"Yes, we were," Meghan said. "I just didn't expect it to end with us streaking down the street. I saw you in the back of his car going down the street. What happened?"

Taylor squirmed in her chair. "He gave me a break. Your clothes, your purses, everything is in my car. I never want to ride handcuffed in a police car again."

"Oh no. He cuffed you?" Meghan shook her head. "You had it worse than we did."

"I've never been more frightened in my life. Sitting in the back of a patrol car, naked, handcuffed."

Meghan shuddered. "That would be bad."

"Instead of taking me to jail, he took me home. Since I wasn't driving, he let me go. If I'd been behind the wheel of a car, he would have arrested me."

Last night after he left, she'd thanked her lucky stars. If not for the sheriff's leniency, it could have ended so much worse.

"Who is the sheriff?" Meghan asked. She turned to Kelsey. "You said before but I forgot."

"My old boyfriend, Ryan Jones," Kelsey said with a laugh.

"And now he's seen me naked," Taylor said shaking her pounding head, remembering the embarrassment of being nude.

Kelsey sighed. "In high school, I went with him for six months. After we got into a public argument in the front yard, my family refused to let me date him. Of course, it was quite a street fight with my brothers right in the middle of it. When the sheriff arrived, my dad convinced him not to arrest anyone. But he told Ryan not to come around anymore. We were done."

"Was that what got you a summer in Europe?" Meghan asked.

Kelsey laughed. "Yes. Later, I heard he went into the military. Never saw him again." Shaking her head, she glanced at Taylor. "How's the big jerk doing?"

"Don't know. We didn't talk too much about him, only me. He gave me quite the lecture." Taylor snorted. "Since high school, I've wanted to dance naked around the statue, but been afraid. Maybe there was a reason to fear the Cupid superstition."

"Dancing around naked in the town square was a little too risqué for me. Until last night when the alcohol subdued my fear," Meghan admitted.

"All I needed was a little liquid courage for me to shed my clothes," Kelsey said with a grin.

"It was kind of fun until the sheriff arrived," Taylor admitted with a giggle.

"Now we test the superstition. Who will find love first?"

Taylor waived her hand and gave a disgusted sound. "I'm not looking for love."

Since the breakup with Kevin, she'd given up finding someone to spend the rest of her life with. At this moment, she needed to focus on the diner. Anything besides finding love and marriage.

"Yeah, well you have a funny way of showing you're not searching for a man," Meghan replied.

"Hey, I can cross off dancing naked in the town square from my bucket list," Taylor said.

"You're a little young for a bucket list."

"Never hurts to start early," Taylor retorted, wishing her head would stop pounding.

The bell tinkled above the diner's door and Taylor glanced up to welcome the new customer. Shock froze her feet to the ground as the handsome, hunky sheriff strolled through the door. The memory of how he'd last seen her caused her cheeks to heat and her chest to squeeze.

Oh no, what did he want now.

❧

RYAN OPENED the door of the restaurant. He'd thought about Taylor all night long as he tossed and turned. The image of her naked body dancing inside his brain tormenting him. The curves on her were enough to make any man make a wrong turn. As he walked in, he saw all three of the she-cats, their heads together whispering at a table. A trickle of fear scurried along his spine making him reconsider why he'd come here.

Just because he'd seen her nude, just because he'd given her a break last night, didn't mean she would go out with him. This morning he'd come here with the sole intent of asking her on a date. Maybe his timing sucked.

Focused on his career for the last three - four years, the time had come to start thinking about dating again. And last night had proven to him a woman in his life would be nice.

Stepping into the diner, he realized he didn't want to confront that table of she-devils. One he'd dated and the other two were her besties. With her partners in crime here, maybe he should wait before he asked for a date.

Like a soldier on duty, he marched up to their table. "Good morning, ladies. Looks like you all survived last night's escapade."

"What are you talking about, Sheriff?" Meghan lied flashing her blue eyes at him. "The cat and I were cuddled up at home, watching reruns."

"Well, I found your clothes, your purse, and your cell phone on a bench in the park."

Meghan clammed up, a mutinous expression on her beautiful face as she flicked back her tawny hair.

"I don't see any bullet holes in your head. You toughed out the military," Kelsey said, a sarcastic tone to her voice.

"Made sergeant and earned several medals," he responded. "And you're looking well. Your brothers still looking out for their little princess."

Kelsey stiffened. "Of course."

"Good to know," he said. "Ladies, I will tell you like I told Taylor. You got a pass last night. But if I ever catch any of you strutting around the fountain, naked again, you'll need a lawyer."

"Thanks for that bit of cheery news," Meghan smarted off.

"Hey, you aren't combing the yellow pages this morning looking for someone to bail you out of jail. The day could be worse."

"I talked them into it," Taylor confessed. "The Cupid statue was my idea."

Lifting her chin defiantly, Kelsey gazed at him. "We're testing the superstition. A scientific study will tell us if Cupid will find us true love. I'll let you know the results."

"It doesn't," he replied. "Remember before you go streaking again."

"Streaking?" Meghan said, her voice echoing in the room. "That fad died in the seventies with my mother's generation."

Facing the auburn haired librarian, he smiled his best strict *you don't want to mess with me* law enforcement expression. "Would you rather I call what you did last night indecent exposure?"

The table grew quiet. Dismissing them, he turned to Taylor. "Are you still cooking me dinner tonight? Do you feel like it?"

Reaching up to her temple, she rubbed the spot. "I'm fine. A small headache. But I'll be all right."

His mind pictured her full breasts, tiny waist, and long legs beneath her white apron and the memory had his heart beating a little faster.

"Be here at seven. I'm going to fix you chicken picante," she said. "It's a new dish I'm trying out."

A grin spread across his face. "So I'm the guinea pig?"

"You'll enjoy the chicken picante. See you later."

Turning, he walked toward the door, feeling like three sets of eyes trained on his back with laser precision. He wished he had one of those new fangled cameras on his vest so he could witness their expressions.

Especially wanting to see Taylor's face.

❦

TAYLOR'S HEART gave a little flutter as she watched him walk out the door, wishing he hadn't said anything in front of her friends. An obligatory thank you dinner for not taking her to jail. Nothing more. Yet, an undercurrent of something more ran between them.

He was in law enforcement. The same career choice of the man she'd found frisking a female officer in their bed. Ryan was everything she didn't want and yet he was exactly the kind of man who made her heart beat like a conga drum, her breathing go haywire, and her imagination run rampant with sexual scenarios.

Therefore, he was a big fat no.

Turning, she noticed Meghan and Kelsey staring at her. "What?"

"You're fixing him dinner," Kelsey asked, a stunned expression on her face. "The man that broke my heart and left me for the military."

"My naked butt is not looking out between bars. What would you have me do? Write a thank you note? Cooking him supper seemed the least I could do."

Shaking her head, Kelsey warned, "He's bad news."

"Hey, I'm the only one last night who said out loud, I'm not searching for love. The rest of you are looking for a man."

"You don't owe him anything," Meghan said while Kelsey just raised her brows.

"After he didn't take me to the pokey, I merely offered to cook for him since he doesn't get many home meals. You guys should appreciate the fact I put my naked butt on the line with the law while the two of you ran off."

Meghan's brows rose. "And who suggested we do the Cupid dance?" Holding up her hand, she said, "But I will say it was good of you to take one for the team. Make sure it's only dinner. Remember your last love interest."

Flipping her straight dark hair away from her face, Kelsey smiled. "A lawman, a cheater, who is on his honeymoon at this moment, celebrating with his cheating spouse."

Taylor sighed. "You're right. Don't worry. I'm not taking Kelsey's seconds. I'm returning a favor and this will be the end of it."

But would it be the end? Attractive in all the right ways, her heart had done a little extra thump when he walked in the door.

And that badge on his chest meant risk. It was a well known fact that law enforcement officers who put their lives in peril often enjoyed the thrill of infidelity.

Kelsey shrugged. "Ryan was my first love and I thought I would die when we ended. He's a risk for women's hearts. He'd break yours as quickly as he shattered mine. Be wary, very wary."

The bell above the door rang and she stood. "The lunch crowd will be coming in soon and I've got work to do. You guys?"

"There is a high school Valentine's dance. I'm one of the chaperones. Ugh."

"Painting is in store for me today. There is still a lot of construction to do before the grand opening. Ya'll will be at the opening? Right?"

"Wouldn't miss it. When is it?" Meghan asked.

"Hell if I know. Whenever my brothers are through with the changes I'm making."

Standing, Taylor glanced at her friends. "Ladies, I had a great time last night, even if it didn't end the way we'd envisioned."

Meghan laughed. "It was fun. Though tonight, the coach and I are the school chaperones. Yuck."

"I'm waiting for the phone call from my brother where his head explodes in my ear."

"Mom and Dad are in South Padre until warm weather reappears or they would have learned about our shenanigan. At twenty-five, I can hear the lecture now."

Tonight, Ryan would come to the restaurant to experience one of her meals. A tiny spark of excitement trickled down her spine. Dinner would include a gorgeous hunk of a man who appeared kind. But lawmen cheated.

❧

TAYLOR WALKED through the restaurant filling coffee cups, talking to the customers, and making certain the waitstaff had exceeded her expectations. Before her parents left for Padre Island, her mother had given her tips on the clients who frequented the diner. She'd told Taylor that Jack came in everyday between breakfast and lunch, alone.

In his sixties, his wife passed away suddenly a year ago and his children all lived hours away.

"Afternoon, Jack," she said, stopping at his table. "How's the food?"

"What do you think?" he said, looking down at his empty plate. "I think you're a better cook than your mother and she's not bad."

"Thank you," she said and wondered how the patrons would accept the gradual changes she had planned for the business in the coming year. If her father let her.

"So what did your boyfriend get you for Valentine's Day?" Glancing down at her hand, he looked back up at her. "No big rock sitting on your finger."

"Yesterday, he married someone else," she said and watched Jack's eyes grow large. "And before you start feeling all bad for me, let me say save that sympathy for her. She's the one getting the loser."

A sympathetic smile crossed his face. "Caught them, did you?"

"Yes, I did, in the act, in our bed," she replied.

"Sit down for a minute," he said and she sank into the chair across from him.

"I told my kids when they were dating, if it doesn't come easy, don't continue. Because once you marry them, it gets harder. So good riddance to your fiancé."

Nodding, she asked, "What about your wife. Did it come easy with her?"

He closed his eyes and she questioned if she should have asked. Then he smiled at her. "Oh, my Margaret was the best. Sure, we experienced good times and bad, but that woman knew the right words to end a fight. I miss her."

"I'm sorry," Taylor said not wanting to make Jack feel worse. "I should never have asked about her."

"No," he said, smiling. "I'm glad you did. No one ever asks me about Margaret anymore. It's like she died and now we can't discuss her. I spent thirty-five years with her and now I can't talk about her?"

"That's sad." Her heart clenched, seeing a smile light up his face, his eyes glowing, his facial muscles relaxing.

"Even our own kids don't mention their mother. Oh, they call once a week to check on me to find out how I'm doing and if I'm still kicking."

Taylor's heart ached for Jack. "She was the love of your life?"

His eyes darkened and she knew he was remembering. "Oh, yes. Margaret made me a better man."

Curious, she leaned in closer wondering how they got together. "Tell me how you met her."

Tilting his head, he stared at Taylor. "You want to hear this or are you just being polite?"

"No, I'm not being polite. I enjoy hearing how people came together."

After her broken engagement and the fiasco of last night, she had doubts about walking down the aisle. Even after dancing naked around the Cupid statue. Not that she believed that nonsense. The time had come to put her childhood fantasies and dreams behind her and concentrate on the family business.

A chuckle rumbled from him as he glanced at her. "We met taking disco lessons."

Taylor couldn't stop herself. She started laughing. "No way. I don't know anyone who could disco dance."

"Yes. We were single, in college, and I didn't want to meet someone at a bar. My buddies convinced me to take a disco class. There was Margaret."

"Can you dance?"

He waved his hand at her like she was crazy and smiled. "Oh no. Years ago, I could, but not now."

"Tell me what happened? Did you ask her out right away?"

"No. We would practice in class and afterwards everyone would go to a club to practice the moves we learned. At the end of the course, I asked for her number so we could go dancing together. Years later, she told me she thought we were just going to be friends. From the very first night I laid eyeballs on her, I wanted to go out with her."

"How long did it take before you went out on a date?"

It was hard to imagine Jack being young and chasing after a woman. Sure, he'd lived in town her entire life, but Taylor never thought much about him and Margaret. They were just a couple her parents' age.

"On the night of the last class, we'd gone to the club. When she decided to leave, I offered to walk her to her car. As we said goodnight, I kissed her."

"Oh, you sly devil you, going in for the kill. What did she say?"

"She was stunned," he said with a grin. "Then she said, 'Wait. Where are you living?' Graduation was looming and eventually, I would return home to Cupid. But I had a few months, so I gave her the name of my dorm. We began to go out and things progressed from there."

"Wow...I can't believe you're a disco dancer."

"Want to see me do the Bus Stop?"

She laughed and noticed new customers had come in and she needed to inquire on the kitchen. "I would love to see you do the Bus Stop, but now, I better get back to work. Mom and Dad wouldn't appreciate it if they came back to a broke restaurant. Have a great day, Jack."

Laying his hand on hers, he patted the back. "Thanks for talking to me about my wife. I miss her so much. Our anniversary was yesterday. Someday I'll tell you how the Cupid statue brought us together."

Taylor froze in her tracks. The Cupid statue? That damn little man with a bow and arrow caused more trouble. Shaking her head, she couldn't conceive marriage would happen to her. Locating a good man was like finding gold in Texas. Hard to find. Maybe a husband wasn't for her.

Almost being arrested. That was more her cup of tea.

CHAPTER 3

*R*yan took a bite of the chicken and the flavors flooded his mouth. The girl could cook. He took another taste and chewed slowly, savoring the spiciness of the salsa and cilantro. Glancing up, he noticed she watched him with a smile on her face.

"What do you think?"

"Your mother's cooking is good, but this chicken is better than anything I've ever tasted at this restaurant," he said, loving the way the dimmed lighting made her face appear soft, her brown eyes shone.

"Thanks," she said. "It's one of the recipes I want to add to the menu."

Staring at her, he couldn't help but wonder why she was still single after all these years. Sure, he'd dated Kelsey, but with her family situation, he'd quickly realized he would never be her man. Leaving for the military had been the opportunity to start fresh away from the watchful eyes of Kelsey's brothers.

"Tell me what happened with the ex," he said curious.

She gave a little laugh. "Simple. Lawmen cheat. What more do you want to know?"

"Well, I don't think you'd told me he was in law enforcement. I will agree there is a statistically higher rate of infidelity amongst officers, but that doesn't mean we all cheat. How did you learn he was having an affair?" he asked.

Giggling, she looked at him. "Easy. I came home from work early and found him and the girl he's now celebrating his honeymoon with having sex in our bed. We had been living together six months, saving money for our celebration of love. He got the wedding and I went to culinary school."

Ryan stared at her, wondering if she was over her fiancé. "How long ago did you break up?"

"Almost a year. Actually, I'm over him if that's what you're asking. As far as I'm concerned, his new wife is the one who got the raw end of the deal."

"Why?"

Shaking her blonde hair, she sighed. "Now I question if he was cheating on a girl when he met me. I'm better off without him and it did give me the freedom to go back to school."

Taking another morsel of the moist succulent chicken with just a hint of spice, he asked, "Is that where you learned to be a chef?"

"Baking has been a love of mine for many years. So when Kevin and I split up, I took my portion of our ceremony money and used it to attend a cooking school. There, I was given the skills and knowledge I needed." She gazed around the family diner. "Someday I'll change up the menu."

Wistfulness shadowed her face. "Is that what you want to do?"

"Yes," she said quietly. "I had been researching opening up my own restaurant in Dallas when my mother called me crying, begging me to come home."

"What was wrong?"

There were a few patrons left in the diner as she leaned in and whispered softly, "My father has been diagnosed with Alzheimer's. They've been planning on traveling the country for years and now they're running out of time. So I'm here and they aren't scheduled to return until next summer."

"Then why not go ahead and make the changes now? Give it a try while they're gone and if it doesn't work on the townsfolk, then you can go back to the old way."

"I considered it."

"Any woman strong enough to dance naked around a fountain in town should have no qualms about trying something new. Unless she's afraid she'll fail."

That was it. Hesitation crossed her face and he wanted to ease her mind. "Look, I'm no food expert, but this is the best meal I've had in months. If the items on your menu are as delicious as this salsa chicken, then you've got nothing to worry about."

Reaching out, he took her hand. "Hot and spicy cuisine, just what I desire. Would you go to the movies with me next week? We could drive into Fort Worth to see a movie and go to dinner."

Tilting her head to the side, she studied him. "Why aren't you married?"

With a shrug, he said, "I'm divorced. Took the vows while I was in the service and then when I came home, she'd created a life without me. After the divorce, I went to college where I dated - but nothing serious."

"Have you ever cheated?"

Frowning, his stomach tightened into a nervous ball. He hated lying to her, but if he told her the truth, she would never give them a chance. Only once in his life had he stepped out on a girl. He'd been young, stupid, and naive to the pain it would cause.

Unfortunately, it had been on her best friend, Kelsey. But Taylor wouldn't be talking to him if she knew. All he wanted to do was explore this attraction between them. "Never."

Licking her lips, she looked down at her plate and then back up at him. "Right now, I'm not dating. You're a nice man, a very intriguing man, but I'm not keeping company with lawmen again."

Releasing her hand, he leaned back in his chair. "But I'm not a cheater."

"I'm not willing to find out."

❧

TAYLOR THOUGHT of Ryan all night long. When he asked her out, she'd been tempted to go to Fort Worth to a movie with him. Sitting across from him had felt natural and the man could get her blood pulsing faster than the mixer in her kitchen.

And when he'd picked up her hand, her heart had sped like a horse shooting out of the gate. Even in high school, one glance from Ryan had warmth spreading through her like an electric blanket on high. He and Kelsey were an item and she wasn't about to poach her best friend's man. Even today, her stomach clenched uneasy that he'd asked her out. Attraction ran between them like a hot wire, but there was Kelsey and she'd refuse to go in difference to her.

The door to the restaurant opened and Jack walked in.

"Good morning," he said going to his favorite table.

She waved at him, knowing what he would order and going into the kitchen to prepare his breakfast. Two eggs over easy, a pancake with a side of bacon. Later he would choose something to go, but his second meal he changed on a regular basis.

Just as she finished cooking, her waitress came in and put in his request. As she hurried out the door, she glanced at Jack's waitress. "I'll make sure he gets his eggs."

She set the plate in front of him and said, "Morning, Jack. How are you today?"

He frowned. "Did I talk your ear off yesterday about my wife?"

"No, I enjoyed hearing about the woman you gave your heart to. I'm a romantic, and love stories like yours and Margaret's always interest me. You only told me how you met her. How long did it take for you to convince her to marry you?"

With a grin, he took a bite. Sighing, he glanced up. "Took me over a year. Margaret had an aversion to going back to a small town. She wanted to live in the big city because she believed a small town's gossip mills could churn out bad news faster than the local TV stations."

Chuckling, he seemed to withdraw inside himself. "For months, I drove back and forth between Fort Worth and Cupid, trying my darndest to persuade her to move. One night on my way to see her, just as I pulled into the Granbury city limits, a tornado struck the small town. Five minutes earlier and that twister would have sucked me up and spit me out who knows where."

"Oh my. What did you do?"

The thought of a tornado spiraling out of the sky in her path was more frightening than a man who cheated. One was a life and death situation. The other, well, once he got caught...

"The road was blocked with debris and emergency vehicles trying to reach the victims. So I turned around and went back to Cupid. Cell phones weren't available, so I didn't talk to her until ten that night. Worried sick, she agreed to move."

Taylor thought about his story and was confused. "You never officially proposed to Margaret?"

"Oh no, I did. Thanksgiving Day at her family's, I asked her to marry me."

"What did you do?" Taylor asked, wondering how the man popped the question to his wife. Was it a romantic gesture or just a let's get married.

Her conscious called her a liar, but her heart knew she'd suffered betrayal at the hands of her fiancé. Not only had he bruised her delicate organ, but he'd injured her pride and left her leery of getting into a relationship again.

"Previously, I'd spoken to her father. Gathered at the table, each person said what they were thankful for. It came my turn and I said how thankful I was for Margaret. In front of her family, I dropped to one knee and told her the only thing that would make me happier was if she would marry me."

Tears welled up in Taylor's eyes. "What a beautiful story, Jack. It gives me hope that there are still men like you in this world."

He lifted his cup to his lips, taking a sip.

"Can I ask you a question?"

"Sure," Jack said. "Depends on what it is as to whether or not I'll answer."

"Did you ever dance naked around the Cupid statue in town?"

A smile spread across his face. "I can't believe that notion still exists. What do you think? Do you think an upstanding man in the community, a rancher, a previous city council member would skip around that symbol, without his clothes?"

Taylor shook her head. "Of course not. Men aren't as gullible as women."

He leaned forward and in a low voice whispered. "A week before I met Margaret, a bunch of my buddies and I were fooling around getting into mischief. On a dare, we decided to test the superstition. Within a year, everyone was wed."

Taylor's eyes widened. "But...but I don't want to be married."

"Well, then, don't dance around the cupid."

With a toss of her blonde hair, she gasped. "Too late. I already did."

RYAN MADE his last drive through town. By the fountain, the bank, the schools, and a few spots where break-ins occurred in the past to make certain everything was legit before his shift ended and his associate took over. As sheriff, he didn't have to do patrols. Sitting behind a desk got boring after a while and he liked to be involved in his community.

Driving by the Cupid statue, he saw Taylor walking. For a

second, he was afraid she was going to stop, but she kept strolling in the dark. Parking the car, he hurried after her.

"Hey, you going dancing again?" he called behind her.

She turned and faced him, her hand to her throat. "You just took ten years off my life."

"Sorry," he said, thinking Taylor appeared stunning. "Needed to check you had your clothes on under your coat."

"My birthday suit is completely covered up," she responded.

"Why aren't you in your car?" he asked almost sad that she was dressed. But then again, he had warned her and he really didn't want to arrest her.

"Walking is good exercise. I stayed later than I intended at the restaurant. Normally, I'm home two hours ago. My choice was either spend the night at the restaurant or walk home."

"Next time ring me," he said, not wanting her to walk alone. "I'll take you home."

"That may go over well here in Cupid, but in Dallas the police department frowns on escorting civilians home. I can hear them saying don't call us on your phone."

"Well, you're not in Dallas, anymore. Anytime you need an escort home, call. Crime is not normally a problem, but you never know who is passing through," he said, enjoying the way the wind tousled her blonde hair. All he wanted was to take her in his arms and kiss her, but he didn't think she would appreciate him exploring her full red lips.

"Come on, I'll walk you home," he said. "It's a beautiful night, even if it is a bit chilly."

Stepping up beside her, they started the short jaunt to her home and she turned toward him. "So Cupid doesn't have a lot of crime and you're not really busy."

"Most of the time. Occasionally, Mrs. Foster's cow gets out and goes wandering down the road looking for sweeter tasting grass. And Mrs. Smith's tom cat likes to cause trouble tomcatting

SYLVIA MCDANIEL

around. Sometimes we arrest a drunk. The busiest time is during football season. If the hometown wins, the mischief abounds."

Smiling, she glanced at him. "Almost ten years since we graduated high school. Seems like yesterday. You and Kelsey, Meghan and Max."

"You and a different guy every week."

"That's not true," she responded. "I didn't date much in school. There was no one serious until college. That didn't last."

Could she be a risk he wasn't willing to take? His first wife had been petty and quarrelsome. He refused to put up with crazy a second time around. Yet, he wanted to learn more about Taylor.

Shrugging, she sighed. "I've never been very lucky in love. I'm way too picky and not inclined to accept a lot of male crap."

"Male crap?" he replied. "What about your part in the relationship stuff. You didn't have a starring role in the drama of why you broke up?"

Huddling deeper into her jacket, he watched the confusion on Taylor's face. Had she never really thought about why her relationships never lasted?

"So, I made Kevin cheat on me? Is that what you're saying?"

"No. He made the decision on his own, but were you having trouble at the time? Did he just randomly decide to choose this other girl and take her home to bed."

Stopping, she turned, her eyes glaring. "You're brave to stand there and tell me it was my fault he cheated."

"I didn't say that. I asked what part you played in your breakups. Do you scream and yell when you fight? Are you too controlling? Do you spend too much money? Are you lousy in bed?"

Taylor began to laugh. "Everything comes back to sex, doesn't it? Men are so focused on getting into a woman's panties, nothing else matters."

"Wait a minute. When you weren't wearing any clothes the

other night I was a polite officer. I treated you with the utmost respect I could a naked woman."

Alluring, gorgeous, full-figured, in the buff woman, which required every bit of his control to maintain his professional demeanor.

"You did. You gave me a blanket to cover myself."

"All right. So what other reasons for your breakups?" he asked. "I'll tell you mine, if you'll tell me yours."

"Oh, so this is a comparison of why we've been dumped?"

"Not exactly, but I do think it shows our weaknesses."

Ryan spent several months in therapy to help him realize what caused his wife to move on without him. The end of his marriage was more than being in the military and overseas all the time. His lack of attention and making her feel preferential and desirable hadn't helped.

Coming home, his need for control when he felt like she'd taken over everything while he was gone had been the death blow. Unable to understand the problem until it was too late, his insistence to be the man of the house killed his marriage.

"Weaknesses? What's that?" she said, eyeing him. "Or maybe I don't want to tell you."

They resumed their casual stroll again, he realized soon they'd arrive at her house. He wanted to end on a positive note.

"Taylor, I'm attracted to you. I want to go out with you. I want to show you I'm not a cheater, but a man who thinks you're an intriguing woman. But I have flaws. I like to protect the people I care about. I want to be the man and you be the soft woman beside me. I want to be partners. And I definitely want to get naked with you."

"Ryan," she said, her voice deep and low, her frosty breath shimmering in the darkness.

"You've been hurt in the past by a lawman. I promise you, I will never cheat on you if you give me a chance."

"That's what you say now, but what about later?"

SYLVIA MCDANIEL

"I'll never cheat on you," he promised.

They arrived at her house and together they walked up the front sidewalk to the door. He leaned in close to her and wanted to kiss her, but could see her eyes had grown large and were filled with wonder and a hint of apprehension.

"I want to go out with you, but I'm not going to ask again. You let me know when you're ready to date and we'll find something to do that will be fun."

Reaching out, he pulled the lapels of her coat tighter and brought her chest against his own. "Night, Taylor. Sweet dreams."

Dropping the fabric, he stepped off the porch and walked back down the street in the direction of his patrol car, grinning. He hoped he'd made an impression on how intent he was about dating Taylor. The woman could ignite his sexual desire with a glance and there was something about her that appealed to him on every level.

Now he had to wait and see if she found him attractive.

CHAPTER 4

*A*fter she fixed dinner for Ryan that one night, he came to the restaurant every day. Even if he didn't eat, he would stop in to say hello and show up again about closing time. It became a habit; he would come by and walk her home. Every evening, she looked forward to their nightly conversations. He'd yet to ask her out again.

She knew he was waiting for a signal from her, and while every time he came near, her heart pounded a little faster, her blood surged through her, and she applied the brakes to her desires.

Being in a relationship for two years that culminated with infidelity didn't make you want to jump into another situation where you could be hurt again. Especially when the man you were considering was another lawman.

In the evening, she'd changed up the diner and now soft lighting, tablecloths, and china gave the place some atmosphere. She wanted to encourage people to try her new dishes on the menu, striving for a restaurant that wasn't just another coffee shop serving pancakes and eggs.

"Good evening," she said to a group of women who came in through the door. "Would you like a table or a booth?"

"Table, please," a middle-aged woman whose demeanor was more like a prominent socialite than some of Taylor's regulars.

"Are you ladies passing through or are you here on business?" she asked, knowing she didn't think any of them were from Cupid.

"We're on the way to a rodeo out in West Texas. Charlene, here, was the queen ten years ago and they asked her to return and present the next crown. Her husband didn't have time to attend, so we're tagging along for the fun, and the cowboys," the woman to the right of Charlene informed her.

"Definitely, the cowboys," another lady said.

Charlene glanced at her. "What do you recommend on the menu."

"The chicken picante is moist and spicy," she told her. "Or if you like something a little on the mild side, I suggest the miso salmon, which has ginger, mirin, miso paste, and cilantro. It's delicious."

"What is miso?"

"A Japanese rice wine," she responded.

The ladies quickly made their choices and Taylor went in the back to cook the dishes while her waitstaff handled the front. She did most of the cooking, but the easier old stuff she let her mother's cook handle. The ones she was trying to build a name for, she created those dishes.

While she was working, one of the waitresses came through the door. "Ryan's here. He ordered the chicken picante," she said.

Since the night she made the dish for him, he came in and requested it at least once a week. She smiled. "I'll put it right on and then I'll go out and talk to him."

After she delivered the dishes to the women's table, Taylor turned and walked away.

Charlene said, "Sheriff, are you busy tonight? My friends and

I are staying at the Cupid Inn. I've got a big empty bed that needs filling."

It was to Charlene's advantage she had her food or she'd find some extra spices cooked in that would keep her going all night long. But Taylor pretended the words hadn't pierced her heart.

"I'm sorry, ladies, but I'm on duty and all three of you have rings on your left hand. A sure sign you're married women and I don't play with fire."

Charlene laughed. "You're right, we're all married. A little fun between friends can't be all bad. We're pretty good at sharing."

"Problem is that I'm not," Ryan said. "I'm a one man, one woman kind of guy. Right now, I'm in hot pursuit of a lady."

Taylor didn't turn around. She didn't acknowledge she'd heard him, if he meant for her to hear his commitment to chasing her, it'd worked. His words were like a cake rising in the oven, fragile and simmering and sending her libido ascending. Still a niggling doubt of uncertainty refused to stop.

Sure, he'd said no to Charlene, but if Taylor hadn't been around would he refuse? If she didn't take advantage of this opportunity would she regret not going out with Ryan? Maybe she should give him a chance. Maybe she was a pushover, but Ryan Jones had just earned himself a date.

৯

RYAN HAD GOTTEN in the habit of walking Taylor the short three blocks to her townhouse after she closed the cafe. The distance was nothing, but she carried the day's cash in her purse and anyone who knew she walked home could take advantage of the situation. With her by his side, he was certain of her safety and it gave them time together.

"Good day at the restaurant?" he asked.

"Yes. How about you? Catch any criminals today?"

He laughed. "No, I wrote three speeding tickets and gave Mrs.

Fletcher a warning for driving without her seat belt. She says it bothers her shoulder and I keep reminding her if she's in an accident the safety harness will save her life. And she says 'I'm almost ninety. How many more years do you think I have?'"

Taylor slipped her hand into the curve of his arm and he glanced at her. This was a first. The touch of her hand on his bicep sent a tremor down his spine. Very nice as his pulse gave a little extra spike. Every night, he fought the temptation to take her in his arms and taste those full lips of hers.

"How did you respond?" she asked.

"I tell her I hope she has a dozen more years, but she won't if she doesn't wear her seatbelt."

"You're such a hard ass," she said leaning into him.

"So what made it a great day at the restaurant?" he said, wanting to understand. She was trying to make some subtle changes and also introduce new dishes, but her clientele were a stubborn bunch who didn't like change.

"We were busy, which is good. But tonight, I overheard a conversation that intrigued me. Did you pay those women to come in and make lewd suggestions in front of me, so I'd know you don't cheat?"

Wow! Her mistrust ran so deep. The urge to kick her ex-fiancé's butt all the way to the Mexican border for what he did to her was strong. "Hardly. One of the reasons lawmen could be known as serial cheaters is because women seem to throw themselves at them. I can't tell you the number of times I get hit on by older, married women who are just looking for a fling. I can see how some men would have a hard time turning it down. Do you think that's what happened with your guy?"

Young and stupid, Ryan let some girl convince him their quick tumble would do no harm. In many ways, Ryan had been lucky. No unwanted pregnancy, no sexually transmitted disease, but a lot of heartache and a painful lesson on the value of fidelity. Never cheat on the woman you love unless you're willing to lose that relationship. Never again, but Taylor didn't know his past and wouldn't understand the reason for his lie.

After they went out, if he saw they had nothing in common, then he'd slink away. But if something was brewing between them that seemed significant and right, he'd confess.

She shrugged. "I don't know. I thought he wanted forever and then I learned he wanted forever, with a side dish of blonde. And she thought he wanted happily ever after with her and I was just a nuisance standing in their way."

He stopped and pushed back a lock of hair that had fallen on her face, caressing her cheek. She gasped and licked her lips.

"I'm sorry that happened to you. In some ways, I'm glad. Because of that terrible time, you returned to Cupid."

She leaned toward him and he took up her invitation. His mouth covered hers and she opened to receive his kiss, his arms pulling her against him. She tasted of some delicious spice she'd used to cook and he savored the flavor. Her breasts were crushed against his chest and he could feel his penis hardening at the way her curves fit snuggly, melding to his muscles.

If they hadn't been on the street and him in uniform, he would have taken the kiss to the next step. He wanted to press against her hard enough for her to know what she did to him. How he desired her.

Leaning back, he let her go, her breathing fast. "Maybe I've been too hasty saying no to you. I haven't been out on a date in nearly a year. Maybe it's time."

He smiled. "What time do you want me to pick you up?"

"How about three on Sunday afternoon?" she said.

Saturday night the cafe had her hustling all night long and he worked a lot of weekends to give his officers a break.

"Perfect. I'll find something special for us to do," he said and gave her a peck on the nose and kissed her again fully on the mouth. When he released her, he grinned. "Sleep well, Taylor."

&

WHAT THE HELL was Taylor doing? In a weak moment, she decided to go on a date with him. Walking her home last night, he told her to dress warmly, but refused to tell her where they were going. Only that it would be fun. He'd walked away whistling and smiling after kissing her goodnight.

And the man could kiss like the devil in blue jeans. When he smiled that devilish grin, her heart pounded a little faster. Something about the way his full lips turned up in a smile that would reach up and spark his dark eyes from serious to playful had her breathing shallow, her pulse racing.

And now they were going out.

The doorbell rang and she took a deep breath, sighed, releasing her nerves. What could it hurt to enjoy his company for one night.

Yanking open the door, he stood there in jeans, a flannel shirt and cowboy boots looking like a sumptuous candy bar. He grinned at her.

"Hi," he said with a drawl that sent a shiver trickling to her center. Drop dead gorgeous. She reminded herself to calm down. She wasn't supposed to be affected by the chemistry oozing from those brown eyes that seemed to melt the clothes from her body.

"Hi," she said. "Do you want to come in?"

"No, we need to get going if we're going to have any daylight."

"What are we doing?"

"You'll see. Did you dress warmly? It's going to be cold."

"I'm layered," she said, her thinking they'd be a good defense against his charm, making it harder for him to somehow convince her to shed her clothes.

"Let's go," he said.

"Zeus, be a sweet puppy," she said as she grabbed her purse and coat and headed out the door.

"Zeus?" he said laughing. "You named a dachshund Zeus?"

"I thought it fitting. A little dog fit to be king."

Ryan laughed as he took her arm and walked her to his car. "Oh, I'm not used to seeing you driving a truck."

"Well, the city kind of frowns whenever you use a patrol car as your personal vehicle. This way we won't have to respond to any emergencies."

"Good point," she said as he opened the door and assisted her in. At first, she was surprised he helped her into the truck. She liked the fact he thought enough of her to treat her special. After all, they were on a date.

As he walked around, she couldn't help but notice how clean and organized the inside of his vehicle looked. Everything had a place, including his phone. Glancing into the backseat, she saw a large basket sitting on the floor board and a cooler beside it.

"Uh, uh, uh," he said, opening the door and climbing into the truck. "No peeking."

The thrill of suspense, kept her on edge, filled with a fun eagerness. He was doing everything to make this a memorable evening.

After starting up the truck, he drove out of town.

"How are your parents," she asked, wishing in all their time walking home together, she'd asked more questions about his family.

"My father passed away three years ago from a stroke," he said softly. "My mother is now living with my sister. Most of the time, I stay in Cupid, but I thought we might go out to the place."

"What about your family? Are they expecting us?"

"Oh, no, they've all moved to the metroplex to make their fortunes."

When you're in high school, you couldn't wait to get out of town and explore the world, but when you became an adult, you couldn't wait to return to the small-town atmosphere. In college, she realized no big city could replace the homey community of Cupid.

"The only place to eat is your restaurant or DQ. I didn't want to drive to Fort Worth today to go to a movie or take you to dinner, so I hope you enjoy what we're going to do."

"What are we doing?"

"We're going out to my parents' ranch."

A warmth sizzled inside her. Years ago, she had gone to a party at his parents' place and thought the house and land beautiful. A meandering river ran along the edge of the property.

"I'm sure you've got something planned," she said, picturing him naked in that big bed of his. Not ready to consider jumping between the sheets with him, her mind went to the thought of the two of them alone at his family home.

The truck turned down a gravel road, bouncing as it hit ruts in the lane. "I would tell you the ride gets better, but it doesn't. My brothers and I are planning on getting out here and fixing this in the spring, but until then, it's like riding a bucking horse."

"Well, now I know what that would feel like. I've often wondered what the attraction was for those cowboys at the rodeo."

"The sensation of being in control on the back of a wild jerking animal for eight seconds. There's no other excitement quite like it. But hitting the ground and getting your breath knocked out of you makes you realize there are safer ways to show you're tough."

"I forgot all about you being on the high school team until now. Why did you give it up?"

"I enjoyed being on the rodeo squad, but I hated slamming onto the ground so hard. When I broke my shoulder, I said enough."

Kelsey had worried about Ryan when a bronc had injured him. At the thought of her best friend, a cringe of doubt raced up her spine. What was she doing here with Ryan? Yes, Kelsey and Ryan's romance happened years ago, but still, the two of them had been the golden couple. The scuttlebutt around school said they were talking wedding dates. And then Kelsey left town unexpectedly.

"What about you? Anything you miss about school?"

Shaking her head there was no question. "Nope. I hated high school. Remember, I dated only a few boys, but never had a steady boyfriend, unlike you."

"Well, I didn't have a boyfriend," he replied.

She laughed. "You know what I meant."

Frowning, he glanced at her before shifting his eyes back to the road. "Did you tell Kelsey you're out with me today?"

All week, she'd fought with herself. One moment she thought she should tell her, and the next, she pushed the idea away. This date could be a complete bust and she refused to ruin her friendship of fifteen years all because of one man.

"No, I didn't tell her," she said.

"Why not?"

"Why ask for trouble?"

"But...why should us seeing one another matter any longer? We had a mutual agreement never to date each other again."

Gazing at him nervously, she said, "I thought you broke up because you went into the military."

"Yes, and she was going to college. Plus, her family believed there was someone better for her than me. Her brothers had been trying to break us up since our first date."

With a chuckle, she threw her hands up. "That sounds like them. I decided today we'd just spend some time together and take it from there."

Nodding, he smiled. "Fair enough. But I'd suggest you tell her soon. She'll need to learn before the wedding."

Taylor felt her head jerk toward him. Her eyes narrowed and she glared. "Not funny."

"I thought it was hilarious. Got you all riled up, like watching a porcupine raise its quills in self-defense," he said, grinning.

"You catch your man in bed with another woman and then tell me what you think about marriage."

He put the truck in park and turned to her. He touched the side of her face with his fingers and smiled. "I don't do men. I like women. Real women like you."

Her heart skipped a beat at the thought of her and Ryan. No, it just couldn't happen. Today was about getting out and dating once again, going for a performance drive. Ryan just happened to be her test vehicle. Time would tell if they reached the finish line or it was a total spin out.

❧

RYAN WAS A VERY HAPPY MAN. Taylor clung to him on the back of the ATV as they rode along the edge of his family property checking the fence lines. When the land flattened out and the trail became smooth, he'd sped up, until she started to squeal. He'd ended their time riding along the bank of the river, watching the water flow downstream, the leaves floating. Overall the afternoon had been fun.

As the sun sank beneath the horizon, he headed the vehicle back to the gathering place in the woods. The place where he'd sat around many a campfire. He always kept a stack of cut logs for whenever he felt the need for some time outdoors.

He slid the ATV sideways as they pulled into camp. As they came to a stop, she laughed, the sound sending warm trickles down his spine.

"You don't drive like a man in law enforcement."

"I've had more training than most people. Not only did the city send us to school, but the marines did as well."

Her arms were still around his waist as she whispered in his ear, "I forgot you spent time in Afghanistan."

He chuckled, the sound snide sounding. That time had been the worst in his life. He never wanted to see that part of the world again. Never. "I'm one of the lucky ones. I lived through that hell."

"Was it bad?"

"Toughest thing I've ever done," he said not wanting to ruin the mood. The afternoon had been great, driving through the trees and being outside in the country air. It'd been the kind of day he enjoyed the most and what Taylor didn't realize today was a test. What did she enjoy doing? Did she like outdoorsy things or was she a girly girl only interested in shopping? So far, she seemed to be having a good time. Now for the final exam.

"Come on, let's start a fire and we can sit back and watch the sun set. In the summer, I bring a tent and spend the night. We could have stayed the night."

She didn't respond and he knew he was pushing things, but the thought of waking up in Taylor's arms was pretty special. And it would happen. Hopefully sooner rather than later. After all the talking, he felt confident a growing attraction was building between them, with her ex-fiancé a brick wall in the way. If only he could plow through that barrier, then she'd be free.

He grabbed the basket and cooler attached to the ATV and placed them on the ground. Walking over to a storage shed, he pulled out some blankets and pillows and handed them to her. "Why don't you set up our picnic area while I start the fire."

She stared in shock at him. "How often do you bring women out here?"

"You're the first. Sometimes I bring buddies of mine. Especially if we're fishing in the morning."

"No chairs?"

He smiled. There were folding lawn chairs stored in the shed, but he wanted something cozier. "Not tonight."

It wasn't exactly a lie. He wanted to sit beside Taylor and gaze at the stars as they came out. Sure, they couldn't be out here too late. But long enough.

"Okay, I'm going to start the fire now," he said, hurrying over to the wood pile. "Need to get it going so the snakes won't bother us."

He kept the space mowed but the cold had sent the snakes into hibernation. In the spring and summer, a smart camper watched for water moccasins or even rattlesnakes.

"Snakes?" she said, her eyes dilating as she gazed around the grassy area. Shaking her head, she laughed. "No, they're gone for the winter."

He smiled. "I think you've been camping before."

"Oh yes," she said, spreading the blanket over the grass and putting out the pillows. "If we brought our rods we could have fished. I love a mess of crappie."

Now, that bit of information he filed for future reference. Frying fresh fish at a campfire under the stars couldn't be beat. The hint of smoke made everything taste better.

"Once it warms up, we'll go fishing," he said, knowing he couldn't wait for fishing weather.

She shivered.

"Are you cold?" he asked, blowing on the smoldering tinder hoping that soon he'd be igniting a fire in Taylor. One that would satisfy them both.

"I'm chilly," she said, glancing at him.

"Wrap the second blanket around you. I'm creating a roaring fire and then we'll eat and watch the setting sun."

"Are you always this romantic?" she asked, cuddling beneath the throw.

"This is my first date in two years. You're the first woman since I moved back to Cupid. Does that surprise you?"

Her mouth dropped open and she smiled. "Why?"

"When I got back from Afghanistan, I needed some time to adjust to civilian life. The Middle East is like existing on two different planets. One is focused on killing an enemy that is hard to recognize, and here, life is work and play and family and living."

She nodded and sank to the ground. "I can only imagine what you saw over there."

"Yeah, not good," he said, needing to somehow redirect the conversation. He added several limbs to the kindling now burning. "After I returned, I made the decision to focus on my career. One of my friends told me Sheriff Fred was retiring and the city was interviewing. I realized going home was where I was supposed to be. I came back to Cupid, applied, and got the job."

He joined her on the blanket sitting beside her. Flames licked the wood and soon heat would begin to warm the space. He pulled the throw around her tighter and opened the ice chest. He took out a bottle of wine and two glasses.

"Wow, I'm impressed," she said, gazing at him in awe.

This reaction he'd been looking for. He wanted her to see how much he was vying for her. With the boys, the small cooler would have held beer, but for her a smooth Chardonnay. Digging in the basket, he found the cork remover.

"I didn't think you drank?"

"I drink. Just not to excess," he said. "It's kind of hard to arrest the town drunks if you show up inebriated."

"True," she said.

He poured the alcohol into the glasses and handed her a wine flute before he scooted closer to her. What he really wanted was to kiss her, but he didn't think now was the right time. "Look at that sunset. In about ten minutes, we're going to be in the dark."

"It appears the sun is disappearing into the river," she whispered. She turned to him. "I'm so glad we did this."

"The night is not over yet. In fact, we have a basket full of food."

"Did you bring s'mores?"

"Yes, I did for dessert," he said turning to smile at her.

She leaned her head on his shoulder. "Thank you. I haven't had s'mores since I was a little girl."

He tipped her glass to his. "To first dates."

SYLVIA MCDANIEL

She smiled and shook her head. "To first dates."

Yet, it didn't seem like a first date. For over two weeks every night he walked her home and every night on the way, they'd laughed and talked and gotten to know each other a little more. They were friends and he wanted to take it to the next level.

The sun slithered below the horizon just as a piece of firewood popped, sending sparks into the sky. "Are you hungry?"

"Starved," she responded. "What did you bring?"

"Well, it's not the gourmet meal you cooked me, but sliced chicken breasts with Brie, grapes and almonds and apples."

"That's perfect. A little protein, some fruit and nuts and who can forgo Brie cheese. I'm very impressed, Ryan."

"This seemed like the place for us to get to know each other better," he said, wanting to kiss her as the first stars appeared.

Instead, he reached into the basket and pulled out the food. He fed her red grapes. With a laugh, she took them from him.

"Remember how Max used to toss grapes in the cafeteria?"

"Oh yes, he got suspended. Hard to believe he played professional football," he said and then it struck him. "Didn't he and Meghan date in high school?"

"Oh yes," Taylor said, picking up a slice of the cheese and stuffing it into his mouth.

"Now she's the librarian and he's the football coach. Wonder if it's hard seeing each other all the time."

Taylor laughed and let him suck a grape from her fingertips. "She can't stand him. They had a misunderstanding that traumatized them both. Now she refuses anything to do with him."

"We were all kids. We made mistakes. I did," he said. "We were learning about relationships."

"Well, maybe you did. Remember, I didn't have a major boyfriend in high school. After college, I thought I had a relationship, but we know how that ended. I'm just not cut out for love and marriage."

"Maybe the right guy hasn't come long yet."

"And you're the right guy?" she asked staring at him.

That taunt was more than he could resist. He pulled her into his arms, unable to wait another moment to kiss. Their mouths centimeters apart and he could feel her heart pounding in her chest. "I don't know. But I'm willing to find out."

He fell back against the blanket, taking her with him.

"Maybe I'm not," she said.

"Or maybe you're scared," he replied, kissing along her ear.

A tremor went through her and he realized her issue. Fear of involvement with another man was keeping Taylor from him.

"Maybe," she said softly, her neck rolling to the side, giving him more access.

"We'll go slow," he whispered.

"How slow?" she asked.

"I won't hit a home run tonight," he said.

She giggled. "You won't even get to first base."

"Well, darn, I hoped to at least cop a feel."

She took his hand and placed it on her buttocks. "That's all you're getting."

"Not exactly what I hoped for, but I'll take whatever I can."

With that, he covered her mouth with his.

CHAPTER 5

*T*he next day, Taylor had awakened thinking about Ryan. The man made their first date memorable and fun, and good Lord, he'd left her hungering for him. Close to midnight, the cold night air forced them to pack up their picnic, put the blankets back in the storage shed, douse the campfire, and ride the ATV back to the house in the dark.

Being in the woods with shadows all around gave a unique atmosphere of both isolation and romantic ambiance. By far, being with Ryan was the most fun she'd ever had with a man. That left her more confused.

He and Kelsey had dated. They'd been an item in school and she couldn't think about hurting her friend. Tossing and turning, sleep had been elusive with thoughts of their night on his family's land and wondering what she should do. Finally, at dawn, she'd concluded that no man was worth losing a girlfriend over.

She couldn't go out with Ryan. It would be breaking the girl-friend code.

The door to the restaurant opened and Jack walked in. "Good morning," he said, his voice upbeat and chipper.

"Morning," she said and hurried over to him. "How are you?"

"I'm doing all right. The sun is shining and it's a great morning."

"Wow, you're in a happy mood."

"My daughter called. She's coming to visit and bringing my granddaughter. I can't wait to see them," he said. "She's the spitting image of my Margaret."

"Wonderful," Taylor said, setting a cup of coffee in front of him. She waited until after the waitress took his order before she spoke. "Do they come often?"

"No. They live in Tennessee, so they only get out here about once or twice a year. She calls me on the phone every week, but I miss seeing them."

"You should go visit them," Taylor responded. "I always loved it when my parents dropped in on me at college."

"Oh no," he said. "I have to stay here and take care of the farm."

Taylor shook her head. He was such a lonely man that she felt sorry for him. She wanted him to find some kind of happiness. "Did you and Margaret ever talk about what was going to happen when one of you were gone? Do you ever think about remarrying?"

He laughed. "Margaret told me if I wanted to marry someone on the way home from the funeral, I had her blessing. She didn't want me to be alone."

"Have you considered dating?"

She couldn't imagine dating at his age, but people did it all the time and if it cured their loneliness, then more power to them.

"How?" he asked. "Most women my age are either happily married or they're man haters because someone did them wrong. And no, I'm not doing that computer matchmaking. I'd never trust a machine to find me a partner."

Nodding in agreement, she said, "I haven't tried meeting men online myself. I'm not in that big a hurry. You will be happy to hear that I went out last night with a man."

His brows rose. "How did it go?"

She sighed. "It was the best date I've ever been on. It wasn't fancy, but rather simple and he went to so much trouble to please me."

"Why do I sense a but coming." Jack laughed.

"Because, there are complications."

"Isn't there in every relationship?"

"Yes, but this is kind of touchy. How do you date a best friend's ex?"

There was more to her reasons for not dating Ryan. Not only was he Kelsey's old boyfriend, but there was the fact he was a lawman, but the biggest reason - he made her feel more than any man she'd ever dated.

His pheromones had her body calling out a response that she wasn't ready to explore. If the last breakup had left her dazed and hurting, what would happen if Ryan ended their relationship?

Wouldn't it be better to end the dating before she had a chance of getting burned.

Jack started laughing. "You don't. But you want to, don't you? When you mention his name your eyes light up. You're not fooling me."

"Yes," she said. "There are other things against him as well. I just don't know."

"Does it matter what other people think?"

She stared at him and she could feel the frown on her face gathering like storm clouds on the horizon. "No. But I don't want to upset my bestie."

"Yet, you want to go out with this man."

"Yes."

"Then tell your friend. She should know you're attracted to her old boyfriend. Maybe she could help you."

"Oh no, I don't think so. Even after all these years, she doesn't like him."

Jack picked up his fork. "You should find out why they can't put the past behind them and move on. You need to seek out the truth from both of them."

It did seem strange that Kelsey, who said she never slept with Ryan, still hated him like the breakup was yesterday. "Enjoy your breakfast, Jack. I think you're right. I should ask some questions."

§

THE DAY HAD BEEN NONSTOP. A steady stream of customers kept Taylor busy in the kitchen. The weekly order of food supplies and meeting with the crazy butcher trying to meet his demands made the day pass in one big blur.

At four o'clock, Meghan walked through the door, her curly hair straight, dark circles under her eyes, her mouth pursed in a frown. Who said being a librarian was easy?

"I need a root beer float," she said, sinking down at one of the tables.

"Coming right up," Taylor said. They didn't have root beer floats on the menu, but when she returned to town, she'd stocked the necessary ingredients. A classic drink for her and her friends. It was good ole Texas comfort food.

Taylor placed the floats on the table and joined her friend. One of the best things about being in Cupid was spending time with her girlfriends.

"Tough day?"

"Since *Coach Max* rescued my naked ass, he thinks we should do all these school events together. As in organizing the spring dance next month. Crowning the Basketball Queen and now he volunteered us as Senior sponsors for next year. He's crawled up my butt so far, he'll need a flashlight to find his way out."

Taylor started giggling. She loved Meghan. This cute little redhead who wore glasses and looked like a Mensa candidate had a sailor's mouth on her. You never knew what would come out.

Sometimes sweet and sometimes a mouthy sassiness that could make her ears burn.

"You shouldn't be laughing. This is all your fault."

"You two have been dancing around each other for months. The Cupid incident brought it all out in the open."

The couple had been hotter than firecrackers on the Fourth of July in high school. And even today, Taylor sensed there were fireworks being lit and was waiting on the big kaboom. But could they overcome their past?

"Well, I would have preferred to sweep Max and our history under the rug. I don't want to deal with the professional jock itch."

"Call his bluff. See if he really will tell the school board about the other night."

"It's not that. Max would never expose me. It's just...I told him the science teacher, Mr. Googly Eyes McBride, has been clingy and doesn't take no for an answer. So today in the teacher's lounge, right in front of the scientist, Max asked what time should he pick me up Friday night."

A private person, Meghan didn't like the spotlight on herself. She'd rather be the wall flower than the star.

"Did the science nerd get the message?" Taylor asked, knowing Meghan didn't want anyone talking about her and Max.

"Yes, it solved my problem with Googly Eyes McBride. More than half the teachers in school were in the lounge eating lunch and now Max and I are the gossips' latest buzz."

The thing with Meghan was that sometimes she liked to play hard to get. But then again, Max and her had a past, a very difficult past. Taylor understood why Meghan wouldn't want the teachers thinking they were a couple.

"Wow, one problem solved, another created."

"Yeah, I feel like I'm wearing a sumo wrestler outfit and we're bouncing against one another. I'm scared to death there will be Velcro somewhere and we'll stick."

"Do you want me to put on a sumo outfit and you can practice with me?"

Her brows raised and she giggled. "You're nuts."

"Drink your root beer; it will calm you," Taylor said, wishing she could confide in Meghan about her date with Ryan. How much she'd enjoyed their simple evening together. How much she wanted to see him again. How much she enjoyed his kisses.

"Thanks," she said, "but I may need something stronger."

Taylor took a bite of the rich float, letting the ice cream slide down her throat. "What can you tell me about Kelsey and Ryan's break-up?"

"Good grief," Meghan said. "We're all back in Cupid. Sometimes I wake up and think we've returned to high school. Are we in a time warp?"

"No," Taylor said, shaking her head. "You're a librarian. I'm a cook."

"Don't make me rethink my career decision," Meghan said, tossing her auburn hair. "After days like today, being a rocket scientist might have been easier."

"I know," Taylor responded, wishing Meghan would answer her question. Sure, they'd all changed since that time years ago, but maybe they had more growing in their future.

For a few moments, they drank their root beer, but Taylor kept waiting for Meghan to tell why Kelsey hated Ryan. "What happened between Ryan and Kelsey?"

Meghan frowned at her over her root beer, studying her face, making Taylor's nerves tighten in her stomach.

"Something went wrong right after we graduated at an end of year party, but I don't know what. Her family whisked her out of town and took her on an expensive vacation to Italy as a graduation present. We didn't speak again for years," Meghan said. "Sorry, I guess I wasn't much help. Why are you asking?"

"Oh, I wondered what happened to the two of them. She hates him."

Meghan's eyes grew wide and she put her spoon down, cursing beneath her breath. "Oh no. You're dating him."

Taylor vigorously shook her head. "No. No, I'm not."

She lied. There had only been one date. They weren't official or anything. One wonderful evening spent together, nothing more.

Meghan sat across the table staring at her like snakes were crawling in her hair. "For some reason, I don't believe you."

"No, Ryan and I are not seeing each other."

After twenty years of friendship, losing Kelsey as one of her besties would devastate her, but being with Ryan was a temptation she was fighting.

❦

AWAKING this morning with thoughts of Taylor filling his head, his body tingling with need, Ryan was anxious to see her again. He didn't want to appear too eager or he feared frightening her away, but last night convinced him he wanted to pursue Taylor.

He wanted to pursue her, catch her, and reel her in, and he aimed to do just that.

Walking into the restaurant before the supper rush, he looked around not locating her. When he couldn't find her, he went into the back. Her employees smiled at him and pointed to her.

He saw her up on a ladder trying to pull down a container from an upper shelf. He hurried over and lifted the box out of her arms. She glanced down at him as she came down the steps. "Thanks."

"No problem," he replied. "Where do you want this?"

"Set it on the floor. I'm looking for the spring decorations. It's time to take down the hearts and cupids and change the flowers."

"Except for your miniature Cupid, right? You wouldn't remove him from the diner."

"Are you kidding me? I'd be run out of town for blasphemy if I removed him from the front. Dad bought that for Mom when they married."

"Did they met doing the Cupid Stupid dance."

"My parents? Very funny. No, they attended the same college. But Dad did propose at the fountain."

"That's better than dancing naked around it," he said, grinning, teasing her.

"We didn't meet at the Cupid statue," she retorted. "We've known each other for years."

Funny, in high school he'd noticed Taylor. But since he was dating Kelsey, he'd avoided the temptation. Now, they were older, wiser and all he could think about was how much he enjoyed her company.

"No, but we renewed our acquaintance in front of the God of Love," he said, wanting to take her in his arms and kiss her senseless.

A stern expression crossed her face, her forehead gathering in a frown. "Don't make anything out of us becoming reacquainted there. Don't give it more meaning."

He smiled, thinking how weird that she was on the defensive and he was the one talking about the superstition and how that curse applied to them. And he wanted the Cupid Stupid dance or whatever people considered it to bring them together.

"I had a great time last night," he said, remembering the fun of being with her. "Would you like to go to Fort Worth this weekend and watch a movie?"

With a shake of her head, she swallowed nervously and he noticed the tenseness radiating from her. "I can't."

"Okay, then how about dinner at my place one night? I'll cook for you." Between midnight and this morning, something changed. She'd been responsive and open and an undeniable connection like an electrical current linked them.

Her blue eyes darkened and she shook her head. "I can't see you again. We can't date."

Disappointment sank like a boulder rolling through his intestines. What happened? They were drawn to one another. Sexual undercurrents ran between them like high wires. So why was she denying them a chance at happiness?

"Why not?"

She sighed, took him by the hand and pulled him into her office where she turned to him. "I can't go out with you. I enjoyed last night, I like you, but you're everything that got me into trouble. You're a sheriff. You dated my friend. It would be strange being with the same guy as Kelsey."

"I was eighteen. We were young, foolish kids, and yes, I broke her heart, but we didn't have sex. I treated Kelsey wrong, but we would never marry. Her family didn't accept me. Her brothers hated me. They didn't want me anywhere near their sister."

Something didn't feel right. He wondered if she knew the truth about why things ended with her girlfriend. Young and naive with raging hormones that just wanted to get in some girl's pants. At a graduation party, he'd made the biggest mistake of his life. Losing his virginity to Rhonda Smothers.

It wasn't his finest moment. When Kelsey learned of his cheating, the shit had hit the fan.

That was the only time he ever was unfaithful. The grief on Kelsey's face, persuaded him to never cause that kind of agony again. If he wanted to screw around, he should have severed his relationship. In his ignorance, he let his drunken dick make the decisions and Kelsey suffered because of his stupidity.

"It doesn't matter you didn't sleep with Kelsey. She's my friend. I don't want to lose her friendship. And you're the type of bad boy I'm attracted to that has broken my heart. I need to end this now before I get a hurt a second time."

There was the real reason. She was afraid. Pain clenched his stomach and yet he needed to back off and give Taylor time.

"There is something special between us."

She wouldn't gaze at him. Even though she denied it, they

shared a strong magnetism. A fire simmered between them, but she was willing to toss this attraction away.

"See you around," he said and walked out the door. He'd experienced a small defeat, but he wasn't giving up just yet. She may have won the skirmish, but he would win the war.

🔖

TAYLOR GLANCED out the door of the restaurant into the black night to see the rain coming down. A flash of lightning followed by a rumble of thunder let her know a very wet, cold walk home awaited her. Her choice was either stay here all night or become soaked. The thought of spending the night at the diner was enough to prod her to move forward. The dog would never understand why she hadn't come home and let him out.

"Guess I better get started," she said, grabbing her coat and bundling up.

The door opened and she whirled around, for a moment frightened and then she saw Ryan. Heat and relief surged through her leaving her heart pounding.

"I thought you might need a ride," he said.

"Thanks," she said breathlessly, warmth filling her at the sight of him. "I appreciate that. I had resigned myself to a cold, wet walk."

"I was in the vicinity and decided to check on you," he replied. "The truck is right outside the door."

The thought of riding in his truck rather than walking in the rain filled her with warmth. Part of her knew she should tell him no, while the other part wanted to ride home with him.

The weak, wanting to stay dry part won.

A flash of lightning had the lights flickering.

"Let's go," she said. "I want to go home and get out of this storm."

Opening the door, he popped an umbrella and held it over her

SYLVIA MCDANIEL

while she locked up. Then he kept her covered while they walked to his personal vehicle. Once inside, he hurried over to his side. Rain pelted the ground so hard it almost looked like hail.

He jumped into the truck and shook his head, raindrops scattering.

"Wow, that's some storm."

"You're not working tonight?" she asked, realizing he'd come to make certain she made it home safely.

"No," he responded, smiling at her. "I traded with one of my guys. I'm off tonight."

They drove in silence until they reached her townhouse. The atmosphere tense and yet oddly filled with want and need.

"Do you want to sit and wait until it stops raining?"

The temptation to stay in the truck with Ryan was strong, but Zeus would be waiting.

"I've got to go inside. The dog hasn't been out since this afternoon."

"Okay," Ryan said and stepped out into the weather. Running through the rain, he reached her side door and held an umbrella over her as she climbed out of the truck. "I think the dog would be smart to hold it a little longer."

"There is only so long he will wait before he leaves me a surprise."

He chuckled. "That's why I don't have a pet."

She gazed at him. "Zeus loves me unconditionally."

"That's because you feed him."

"And love on him and play with him and take him for walks. He's not too fond of me when I give him a bath, but he smells a lot better."

They reached the door and she unlocked it with her key. "Watch out. I don't let him out without a leash. He's been known to take off running and there's a pit bull that lives three doors down. They don't like each other very much."

The porch overhang kept them dry and yet the wind blew

64

with gale force, blowing her hair in her eyes. When turning the knob, a gust grabbed the door from her hand sending it flying.

Zeus darted out the open portal, running with wild abandon. Rain still came down in sheets and lightning made a crackling sound in the night sky.

"Oh no," she cried. She tossed her purse inside the house and took off after the wayward mutt.

"Wait," Ryan yelled.

But she couldn't quit chasing after the animal. If she did, Zeus would be two blocks down the street.

"Zeus, stop," she commanded in her strongest "mind me" voice.

She glanced at Ryan as he ran beside her. "I'll try to get in front of him."

All she could see was a dachshund in a full out sprint, his ears flapping in the wind and his tail straight like a pointer. Thank goodness there was no traffic as he crossed the first street.

"Stop," she screamed and he kept going.

Swirling water rushed down the road flooding the area. "No. Stop. Zeus."

The rushing water picked up her dog and she watched his head go under, her chest tightening with pain. Fear of drowning halted her at the edge as she stared in shock at his little legs working to keep his head from sinking in the water.

"Oh my God, he's being swept away," she screamed, terror paralyzing her.

"Stay here," Ryan said. "I know where I can reach him."

He ran down the street to where a bridge went over the stream that was normally a trickle. Thunder boomed around them. Ryan stepped out onto rocks on the side of the bank. For a moment, he vanished and her chest squeezed painfully; horror exploding within her.

What if Ryan was hurt or even killed saving Zeus? What if Ryan drowned? What if she lost both of them?

Tears welled up in her eyes and she couldn't stop her feet from moving. She moved toward him, afraid of what awaited her. Her heart pounded in her chest, aching as fear pumped adrenaline through her bloodstream like the flood waters swirling around her.

The top of Ryan's dark head of hair came up out of the drainage ditch and relief made her knees weak. In his embrace was her beloved Zeus. Unable to stop herself, she ran to Ryan and wrapped her arms around him as Zeus licked his face and chin. She pulled him to her, the dog between them.

"Thank God, you're all right. I was so scared. I thought I'd lost both of you."

Ryan put his arm around her. "We're okay. This damn mutt of yours is a pain in the butt, but he swam right to me. I swear he was grinning when he saw me. He's shivering and shaking and so happy to get out of that water."

She laughed and ran her hand through the animal's wet fur. "He is a pain, but a lovable, sweet dog and I don't want to lose him or you," she said softly staring up into his brown eyes.

The sky illuminated and thunder shook the ground near them, letting them know the storm was far from over. "I think we better go back to the house."

With a secure grip on her beloved pet, he took her by the hand and they ran back to her condo.

As they stepped inside the door, he set the puppy on the floor. Zeus gave a good shake, sending water droplets spraying like a sprinkler.

Taylor stared at Ryan, who dripped water on her floor, but she didn't care. At the realization of what he'd done, her heart was filled with gratitude.

"Why don't you go in the bathroom, remove your clothes, and I'll put them in the dryer," she said. A practical suggestion, but the implications had her pulse pounding, her body warming. The thought of him naked in her house was enough to start a sensual fire roaring through her.

"What do you suggest I wear while my clothes are drying?" he asked. "Maybe I should just go home."

She shook her head, not ready for him to leave. "No. It's still storming. I have some large towels that you could wrap around yourself. Or I have a fluffy bathrobe, your choice."

His brows drew together in a frown. "What color is the bathrobe?"

"Pink," she said with a giggle.

"Just what I thought. I'll take my chances with the towel."

This afternoon she'd told him she couldn't date him again and tonight he'd driven her home, saved her dog, and would be in her living room nude except for a towel. Life was certainly full of surprises.

CHAPTER 6

*R*yan stepped out of the shower. The hot water had warmed and refreshed him. Drying off, he searched through her cabinets for yet a second towel and circled it around him. This wasn't exactly how he planned to spend his night, but the thought of them both being naked was enough. He had to tell his junk to power down.

They were riding out some rough weather together, alone, and without any clothes. With his fingers, he combed his hair before he walked out of the bathroom. Taylor sat in the living room, the fireplace burning, Zeus in her lap as she rubbed the dog's ears.

"You scared me tonight," she said leaning over him, her blonde hair falling to cover the dog's face. She glanced up and saw Ryan standing in the doorway. Her eyes casually looked him over and when she noticed the towel, she swallowed. "Thanks for rescuing Zeus. He means a lot to me."

"You're welcome," he responded, nodding, he sank beside her on the couch, hoping the damn towel didn't start to rise. In yoga pants and a T-shirt without a bra, she'd never looked more beautiful.

"I feel overdressed," she said with a sigh.

Why did it seem they were determined to get naked together? First Taylor and now himself without clothes?

She swallowed nervously. "I put your things in the dryer."

"Thanks," he said.

Zeus jumped down and went over to his bed next to the fire and immediately curled up.

"I think he's worn out."

"He should be. His little legs were treading water, working hard to keep that long nose from going under. I grabbed him by the collar as soon as he was in reach. He's a lucky dog."

A tear trickled down her face and he reached over and swiped it away. "It's over. He's safe."

"But I could have lost Zeus. You could have died. I've never been more frightened," she said, gazing at him with those blue eyes that seemed to wrap around his heart.

"I'm happy you were concerned about my safety, but the water was only about three feet deep. I was worried about your pet."

She turned and face him. "Not many men would have taken the risk you took for a dog. I'm glad you're okay and now he's napping off the excitement."

A brilliant flash of lightning sparkled and with a popping noise, the lights went out. She leaped into his arms. "That was close."

The touch of her body crushed against his chest was his undoing as his penis begin to harden and swell beneath the towel and he realized soon there would be a tent below his waist.

Laying her head on his shoulder, she clutched him. "Yes," he said, the clean scent of Taylor creating havoc with his senses. "I don't think my clothes are going to dry."

"No," she whispered softly, her breath tickling his ear. "I should get candles."

She started to rise, but he stopped her. "No. Leave it."

He didn't want her getting up. He liked her right here in his lap and felt her stiffen the moment she felt his hardened dick against her leg. Her face turned toward him, her eyes round and wide in the darkness had his heart juddering in his chest. Her mouth descended on his.

The smell of something sweet and musky and feminine enveloped him as awareness prickled over his skin like butterfly wings. The heavy throb of his blood gathered in his loins as her mouth covered his tentatively.

His hands slid to either side of her cheeks, bringing her in tighter, closer, as he took over the kiss, consuming her lips, sliding his tongue between her teeth.

With a moan, he sucked on her lips, wanting to consume her very essence. A fiery response rose inside him and he pulled her down as he lay back on her divan, his mouth never leaving her. Pulling her snug against him, her breasts smashed against his chest, his cock hard against the vee of her legs, he gripped her face tightly.

There was so much more he wanted from this woman. He wanted to stroke her intimately, feel her body warm and responsive to his caress, to watch her shatter under him and cry out his name. And yet he had to remind himself to take it slow. Surrounded by the sensual overload from the woman on top of him, it was difficult to consider slowing the pace.

Sighing, she released his lips. "Ryan."

Unable to stop the need within him, he flipped her onto her back knowing he would halt when she told him to. The towel got caught on a sofa cushion exposing his buttocks.

She reached back, her fingers trailing down his cheeks, sending a flash flood of heat searing through him. "Taylor," he groaned and yanked the material away. He ground his hips against her center and she gasped.

"I want you," he said, remembering the nude woman shivering in front of the Cupid fountain. Since that day, she'd been like a craving, a compulsion, a desire he wanted to fulfill. Something about the connection between them seemed primitive. Sexual. And so much more. He wanted to explore life with Taylor, only this woman, no-one else, and that scared him.

With a yank, she pulled her shirt up. When he grasped what she was doing, he helped her remove the garment. Braless, he was past the chance to stop from sampling her beautiful breasts. Leaning down, he took her puckered nipple into his mouth, sucking on the orb while his hand caressed her. Nipping the kernel of her breasts with his lips, he went between her rounded globes hungrily devouring the soft mounds.

"Ryan," she groaned, her eyes beseeching him.

Did she want him to halt and put an end to their lovemaking? He prayed that wasn't so, because it would kill him to walk away from fondling her when he was so hot and hard.

"Grab a condom," she said with a moan, her mouth weaving a trail of fire across his chest.

The woman was smart. He stretched his hand out to where earlier he'd emptied his pockets on her coffee table, he reached for his wallet and pulled the packet out.

Rolling to the side of the sofa, he ripped the package open. Before he could put the rubber on, her hands glided up and down the smooth skin of his dick.

His hand halted her movements and while he slid the condom over his manhood, she removed her pants and underwear.

Staring into her eyes, he laid on top of her, feeling the way her body seemed to fit his in all the right places. Fire raged through him at the feel of her skin against him. Her satiny flesh flowed like silk over him as she moved, stroking the fires raging wildly through him. Running his fingers between them, he found her slickened folds, the evidence of her desire coating his digits as he teased her until her breathing was ragged.

She grabbed his face pulling his lips down to her own, punishing him with her kiss as she clung to him, lifting her hips to show him her need. With a groan, he answered her call, pushing himself inside until he filled her completely. Hunger and rapture overwhelmed him as he pounded into Taylor, branding her as his own. Filling her, touching her soul, he gazed into her eyes and understood instinctively he'd known it would be like this with Taylor.

Staring into her blue eyes, he became entranced as together they soared, every nerve exploding with a pleasure centered in this woman.

"Ryan," she cried as her body shuddered and with one last thrust, he followed her over the edge, crying out her name as they clung to one another.

Tumbling back to earth, triumph oozed from every pore. Sex had never been this great with any other woman. Taylor Braxton's Cupid spell had bound him to her and he hoped and prayed it was forever.

֍

TAYLOR ROLLED over and hit a hard, warm male body in her bed. With startling reality, she opened her eyes to see Ryan curled on his side, completely nude. She looked down and realized she was naked and then every detail from the night before flooded her brain like the storm that slammed the town last night. Only this was her own personal thunderstorm.

Ryan, her best friend's ex, slept soundly next to her in bed. And while she should feel some remorse, she only had happy memories of last night. The sex between them had been meltdown fantastic. Something Taylor never experienced before. Yet, why did it seem like she was cheating on her friend.

Ryan stirred and she didn't know what to do. Part of her wanted to curl around him and go for a second or third or fourth round, while the loyal friend inside her said she'd created a disaster. How could she ever look poor Kelsey in the face again without knowing she'd done the deed with Ryan.

The phone rang and she glanced at the number. No! It couldn't be. Not this morning. She answered.

"Hi, Taylor," Kelsey said. "I'm meeting Meghan for breakfast and thought maybe you'd like to join us. She has some gossip she wants to share."

Inside Taylor groaned, praying that chatter wasn't about her and Ryan.

"I can't," she said stuttering.

"Is everything okay?" Ryan asked.

She turned and shook her head at him, frowning. She didn't need for Kelsey to hear about her and Ryan this way.

"Do you have someone there with you?" Kelsey asked.

"No. It's the television. I turned it down," she said, staring at Ryan who suddenly was all smiles.

"Well, we're going to meet up in about thirty minutes," she said.

Taylor really wanted to visit with her friends, but Ryan was here and they obviously needed to talk. "Let's try to have dinner together one night soon."

"Sure. That sounds good. I'll tell Meghan you can't make it and if she tells me any juicy news, I'll give you a call."

"Great. I'll talk to you later," Taylor said and pressed the end button.

She breathed a sigh of relief as Ryan's arm snaked around her, pulling her down in the bed with him again.

"I gather one of the girls wanted to get together?"

"Yes, Kelsey," she said stiffening under his touch, feeling guilty for enjoying the pleasure she found in his arms.

Turning on her side she faced him. "Hey, I like you a lot. I really do, but we can't do this right now. I can't be with you."

"We're back to that again. I thought last night we'd made progress. I thought you enjoyed being together as much as I did."

She bit her lip. How could she deny the euphoria the two of them had generated? At times, she worried the neighbors would

73

complain or call the sheriff, only to find out he was in her bed. "I had a wonderful time."

Unable to control herself, her hand reached up and brushed a swipe of his curly brunette hair away from his face. Even now gazing into his brown eyes, her body lit up like a power unit. She wanted him again and again and again and that wouldn't stop her from acquiring a broken heart. Did she enjoy a lawman crushing her soul?

"Is this about Kelsey," he asked. "What we shared was special. I'd like for this to be more than a one-night stand, but if you're going to keep insisting we can't date each other, I can tell you I'll get tired of that real quick."

"I can't help it. We've been friends since grade school. You were hers first."

"Oh, come on, Taylor, that was six years ago. We've both moved on or at least I have."

"Then why does she hate you so badly?"

Ryan's stomach clenched and he feared this conversation couldn't be good. He didn't like that he lied to Taylor about cheating, but he wanted to see where this attraction went. With Kelsey, he'd been a young, stupid teenager more interested in getting into some girl's pants for the first time than realizing the pain he caused his girlfriend.

"Would it help if I spoke to Kelsey?" he asked not wanting Taylor and Kelsey to talk about him, hoping he could ward off the coming storm he despaired would soon erupt over him.

"No," she said. "I think we should keep what happened last night to ourselves. Let's give this more time. If it develops into something more, then when I think she's ready to hear about us, I'll tell her myself."

And Ryan knew then all hell would break loose. While he didn't like hiding their relationship, no matter which way he went, a truckload of trouble waited for him. He should probably confess now to Taylor the reason Kelsey hated him, but this felt so good he didn't want it to end. Not yet.

There was no way to keep this information hidden from her. Sooner or later, she would learn what he'd done and when she did, her trust would go up in flames. Evidently, it didn't appear he'd learned from his past mistakes. Because if he had, he would have been honest with her right up front. Yes, he cheated - one time.

❧

TAYLOR MET the girls at Valentino's Bar and Grill. The last time they'd been here had been the night they danced drunk in front of the Cupid statue. Tonight would end differently.

"We're all together again," Meghan said hugging her.

"Where have you been?" Kelsey said. "I don't see you very often."

"Working. I don't leave the restaurant most nights until after ten. By that time, I'm exhausted."

They sat at a table in a quieter area of the bar and gazed at each. "I'm not letting you girls talk me into anything foolish tonight," Meghan said. "I'm still paying for that stunt."

"Me too," Kelsey said.

"What about you, Taylor. Ryan still coming around?"

They both looked at her expectantly. "Occasionally, he comes into the diner. But tell me about you girls."

No way would Taylor discuss Ryan with Kelsey. Not now. Maybe not ever, but at this moment, she didn't want to know what happened between her and Ryan. She feared he and Kelsey had sex while they were together in school. The thought of being with a man who'd slept with her friend was well...icky. So she wanted to be oblivious for as long as possible.

"Coach Max and I are battling it out. The man has some nerve. He's still mad at me about high school. I don't understand."

Taylor shook her head. "Men."

"I think from now on we should all forget that we knew each other back then and start fresh. We've all changed. I have," Meghan replied.

"Not me," Kelsey said. "I'm still the spoilt little princess or at least my brothers think so. You'd think I was nine years old instead of twenty-six. But now the idiots are pushing me toward Cody. My oldest brother told me he would make me a fine husband. Like that's going to make me want to go out with the man."

"I thought you liked him," Taylor said.

Kelsey sighed. "I do. I just don't want anyone to push me, especially my family. He's their best friend. It would be like me convincing one of you girls to marry one of my rowdy siblings."

Meghan laughed. "Your brothers are handsome men, but they're a little too bossy for my taste."

"Nice guys, not for me," Taylor responded laughing. "I know too much about them."

"Exactly," Kelsey said. "Do you want to date a man you saw running around in his Superman underwear, playing games? Not an image that gets me all hot and bothered."

"But you're interested, aren't you?" Meghan said.

"Meghan, you are way too perceptive," Kelsey said with a sigh. "Abs of steel, a trim waist, and the darkest emerald eyes that when they look at you, seem to start a fire in your belly. But I'm fighting this all I can. My family loves him. That's a strike against him right there."

Taylor laughed, wishing she could share her new feelings, knowing it would ruin the evening if she did. "I'm happy for you."

"Don't be happy for me. Warn me, tell me to run."

"Tell Ryan--" Meghan stopped. "Speaking of the devil, there he is."

Taylor's head almost spun around in a complete circle as she glanced behind her.

"Hello, ladies," he said. "I hope you girls are staying out of trouble. Don't let Taylor convince you it's a great night to dance around the Cupid statue," he said.

She frowned and shook her head. "Hardly. Someone promised to arrest us if we did that again."

"I'll be waiting down the street with handcuffs if you want to test me," he said as he tipped the edge of his hat and walked away. "Duty calls."

Kelsey watched him walk away while Taylor refused to turn and glance at him. She wanted to. Oh, how she wanted to know if he was watching her. She wanted to run out after him and tell him to meet her at her house at midnight. She wanted to pull his luscious mouth down to hers and explore it one more time. Picking up her phone, she started typing.

"I'm so glad you didn't start dating him," Kelsey said.

Taylor jerked her head up from her lap where she was just about to send a booty call message.

"Why?"

"In high school, he partied a little too much. Part of the reason we broke up," Kelsey said.

But that was years ago and people grow or go off the deep end or even go backwards. Earlier they'd discussed how much everyone had settled down in the years since school.

"You need to find someone to date," Meghan said staring at Taylor. "We're both busy and I don't like the idea of you being alone."

Taylor sighed. "I don't have time for a boyfriend. We've all changed in the last seven years, hopefully for the better. I'm more responsible now. I don't want to be the person I was at eighteen. I want to be someone unique. Someone better."

Pausing, she didn't send the text. She waited. Why was she letting the fact he and Kelsey were once together rob her of a chance for happiness? Maybe the time had come for them all to get over being young and stupid. Maybe this was part of growing up, accepting a person for who they were today.

Twelve o'clock my house. She sent the text, wanting to see him again. Missing him so much, she ached.

He replied. *I'll be there.*

CHAPTER 7

$\mathcal{R}$yan's body warmed, his dick grew hard at the sight of Taylor's text message. He got off work at ten and that gave him plenty of time to go home, shower and prepare for his date. Though he knew it was only a booty call.

He didn't like hiding from everyone. If they were going to have a relationship, he wanted it out in the open for people to see, otherwise it appeared tainted.

He'd experienced that feeling once and never wanted to go there again. Not even for Taylor.

Hours later, he rolled off Taylor and pulled her in next to him. She snuggled up against his chest.

"That was wonderful," she said her breath coming out ragged.

"Not bad," he said, wondering if she really meant it or if she was using him for sex. It had never happened to him before, but he longed for so much more with her. And currently, he wasn't getting what he needed.

"So tonight was just a booty call," he asked.

She raised onto her elbows and glanced at him, her brows furrowed. "What makes you think that?"

"Did you tell your girlfriends we're dating? We're in a relationship?"

He watched her bite her lip, and knew she hadn't. Flipping over to her back, she stared up at the ceiling. "I'm not certain what we're doing."

"We're having sex on a regular basis. This is the third time this week," he said. Part of him felt hurt she would keep them secret from the people in the small town. He didn't like sneaking around like they were having an illicit affair.

"Are you complaining?"

"Hell no. But it's not right. I don't want to be your booty call guy. I don't want to hide from your friends. I want to take you out and show you off."

"That's because you don't have to worry about losing friendships. I do."

Sitting up in bed, frustration pulsed through his veins. "I want to be a normal couple. I don't want to sneak over here at night."

"You're not," she said. "I told Jack about us."

"But you didn't tell Kelsey or Meghan."

"No, I didn't," she said getting up and grabbing a robe lying on a chair nearby. "I'm waiting for the right time."

Why was he arguing with her over this? Once she told Kelsey, she would unload all the details of their break-up and then Taylor would learn about his lie. The tension and growing vexation between them couldn't be good.

Rising, he pulled on his underwear and pants. "It makes me think I'm being disrespectful to you. It makes me think I'm using you and I never would do that. I care too much about us."

At the door, she turned and walked back to him. She slipped into his arms and he wrapped them around her. Warmth spread through him like fire and he wanted to take her back to bed, but the time had come to leave.

"I don't think you're using me. I'm just not ready to tell the world. I want to make certain this is going to work. You have to remember, I'm the girl who until a year ago, was engaged to be married. I don't want to make another mistake."

How could he argue with her when she used logic? In a twisted kind of way, she was protecting both of them. In a small town, the gossips could torture you. She wanted to be absolutely sure before they went public and let the rest of their friends know they'd found each other.

But he wouldn't wait much longer. Concealing seemed wrong and he wanted nothing to do with anything unseemly.

"Soon," she said. "I promise you once I'm convinced, we'll let everyone know we're a couple."

Part of him wanted to shout to tell the world that Taylor was his girlfriend, while a smaller part realized his history with Kelsey would cause them trouble. Lots of trouble. So why did he continue to push the boundaries?

Because he cared.

𝕚

TWO DAYS LATER, Taylor saw Jack come through the door of the restaurant. For nearly a week, they hadn't been able to talk. She walked out of the back and hurried to his table. "Good morning," he said, smiling at her. "You look all bright and chipper."

"The sun is shining, we've had some rain, and I'm hoping spring is on the way," she said.

"Calving season started and I've already lost two babies. I just hate losing the babies. Makes the momma cows very sad. Makes me feel bad for them."

"Oh dear," she said and sank into the chair across from him.

"It's part of being a rancher, but still, it's damn frustrating when you don't understand why Mother Nature took the little one."

"How did your wife help you handle disappointments like this whenever they happened."

He laughed. "She cried whenever we lost one of the animals. I would hold her while she sobbed. Afterwards, she would get the ice cream and fix us banana splits. Margaret got down, but she never stayed there. Right up till the time they gave her the cancer diagnosis. Then she wasn't depressed, just sad. She kept telling me she was worried about leaving me behind."

"You've done all right," Taylor said not really sure, but wanting it to appear she thought he was a strong man. He gave that appearance anyway.

Shrugging, he looked down at the plate the waitress had placed in front of him. "I do all right. While I appreciate your company and the restaurant's cooking, I miss Margaret's. I miss her chicken enchiladas. The woman's food could rival any diner."

She smiled. "I'm here all day and yet I'm so tired on the weekend from working, I don't cook. There's nothing like a home cooked meal."

"How did you do in the storm the other night. That was quite the doozy."

Taylor glanced at the older man. She needed someone to confide in. Someone other than her girlfriends who would never understand. She felt so confused about Ryan.

"Ryan came by and took me home so I didn't have to walk," she said with a sigh.

Jack's brows rose. "That was a heavy sigh. What happened."

With a flip of her hair, she told him about how Zeus had almost drowned and how Ryan risked his own life to save her dog. The dam seemed to break and she confessed to Jack while drying Ryan's clothes the electricity went out and somehow they found themselves in her bed.

Normally, she wouldn't tell a stranger about her love life, but Jack was a friend. A confidant, and at this moment, she desperately wanted a friend to help her feel less perplexed.

"So why so pensive? Do you regret being with Ryan?"

Closing her eyes, she thought about their time together and knew it wasn't regret that had her unable to sleep at night.

"No, I miss Ryan. I want to spend more time with him. He fills a missing space in my heart, and that both excites and frightens me. We've seen each other nearly every night this week."

Nodding, Jack finished his eggs and pushed his empty plate away. "So what's holding you back?"

"My friend Kelsey, she used to date Ryan."

"So?"

"She hates him. She's warned me about him."

"Have you ever asked her why she's warning you about him?"

"I'm afraid. I'm not sure I want to know. Whatever it is happened when they were dating in high school. I asked my other girlfriend, Meghan, but she had no idea."

He shook his head. "You need to talk directly to Kelsey. You need to learn what happened before you go much further."

Taylor picked up her coffee and nodded her head. "I know. I know, but I'm frightened of what I'll find out. I have put this off as long as possible. I like Ryan a lot and I don't want it to end. But I also realize he's getting frustrated because I won't allow him to go public with our romance."

"Sometimes fear of the unknown is worse than what you find out. Deal with the problem so you don't lose Ryan."

❧

TAYLOR GLANCED around the table at her two friends. Since they'd all returned to town, they were making it a habit to have dinner or drinks at least once a week at Valentino's Bar. The country music twanged in the background as they sat around reconnecting.

"Anyone want to go to Dallas with me day after tomorrow?" Kelsey asked. "I've got to attend market and I could use the company."

"Can't," Meghan said. "I've got school."

"I would love to, but I have to stay here and run the restaurant," Taylor said with a sigh, knowing she missed her parents being here to help keep their business going. But they deserved this winter away. Soon, they would be retired and while she wished the other members of the family would help out, she didn't really anticipate that.

"We should plan a girls' trip," Taylor said, knowing her employees could handle the restaurant for one night without her.

"Yes, spring break is coming up in the next week. Let's go to the spa," Meghan said. "I'm feeling the need to get rid of some old dirt."

Kelsey laughed. "Would that dirt go by the name of Max?"

"Hell, yes," Meghan said shaking her head. "The man knows how to wind up a girl. I can't believe he's inserted himself into my life again after all these years."

"You're welcome," Taylor said, knowing she was the reason Max was back in Meghan's life. Part of her felt guilty that he'd been the one to pick her up the night they did the Cupid Stupid routine, but the other part thought Meghan still loved him. And if that was true, she hoped they could work things out.

"Okay, so one week from this Saturday we're going to the spa for spring cleaning," Kelsey said.

"I'll make sure my employees know they are in charge," Taylor said, a trickle of excitement going through her at the idea of the three of them spending the day together.

"I'll make the appointments and the hot massage guy is mine," Kelsey said.

"Great! She's already laying dibs on the only man we'll see," Meghan said.

"Do you want him?"

"No, but it seems you always get the hot, sexy ones," Meghan replied.

"Girls, I don't want him either, so Kelsey can have him," Taylor said.

Kelsey laughed. "I'm the only one who doesn't have a hunk chasing after them and you guys get upset because I called dibs on the masseuse?"

A frown formed between Meghan's brows. "I don't have a hot guy chasing after me."

"I don't either," Taylor said, appearing surprised.

Kelsey shook her head. "Meghan's been complaining about her ex being back in her life, and you," she turned and faced Taylor. "I've heard rumors that a certain sheriff in town is hot on your trail."

"Not mine," Taylor said, knowing it was a complete lie. Her cheeks grew warm just thinking about the night she'd spent with Ryan. She'd never had such a great sexual experience in her life. Never, and yet, she was afraid of getting permanently connected to yet another lawman.

"Then why is his patrol car seen a lot of nights in front of your townhouse?"

Nothing was secret in this town. Nothing. "Because he often walks me home or takes me home from the restaurant. I am carrying the night's receipts with me."

"Why don't you drive," Meghan asked.

"I could, but look outside. I'd have to put a lot of nickels in those parking meters because there is no parking in the back. Not unless I want my car sideswiped by a delivery truck."

Kelsey stared at her intently like she could see inside and knew she was lying. Somehow she needed to change the discussion. "He's trouble, Taylor."

What could she say? She wanted to ask Kelsey what happened between them that left her so bitter. But they were in a crowded restaurant filled with her clients who sometimes had large ears and even bigger mouths. This conversation was more appropriate in a small quiet setting. Besides, the only thing happening between her and Ryan was sex. A lot of really great sex. Nothing permanent or even temporary other than using each other's body.

And her conscious immediately twinged, sending a shudder through her.

"Our sheriff has been doing his duty by making certain I arrive home safe and sound. Nothing more. Not like Miss Meghan who is sitting over there with one of the greatest NFL players chasing her."

"He's retired. And he's nothing more than a high school football coach who I share a disturbing past with."

"And he'd like to make it your future as well," Kelsey said.

"Maybe. But maybe not. Either way, it doesn't matter because I don't want a future with him. We have too many trust issues to try to resolve and I'm over him. What about you, Kelsey? You've not said how your brothers reacted to hearing you were streaking through town."

A heavy sigh released from her. "I'm not certain what is going on. My brother's friend Cody picked me up, remember? But so far he's kept quiet. You know, if he wasn't my brother's best friend, he might be kind of nice. But dealing with my brothers is way more than I want. Yet, Cody is a nice guy. He's been coming over and helping me in the shop."

"Whoa, there," Meghan said. Her brows drew together in a frown. "You've known this man for twenty years and you're telling me he's suddenly a nice guy? Last time we were all together, you were talking about his Superman underwear."

"Well, he's nice. He even kissed me the other day, but I could never get seriously involved with him. He's my brother's best friend. They would know *all* our business."

Meghan shook her head. "Not buying it. You like Cody, but you're afraid."

"Am not. I kissed him."

"On a scale of one to five with five being a really great kiss, tell us what you thought," Taylor said knowing she was putting Kelsey on the spot, but sometimes you had to with this girl.

"It was a six," she said quietly.

"Oh," Meghan said. "There is more to this story."

"No. It cannot happen between me and Cody. Jim would love it and he'd think he had control over me."

"Who gives a crap about your brothers. You worry way too much about them," Meghan said.

"She's right," Taylor said and it smacked her in the face like a two by four. She worried what Meghan and Kelsey would think of her dating Ryan. She was the biggest damn fool. Just then the bell over the door rang and she glanced up.

Sheriff Ryan walked in the door and headed straight for their table. She was in so much trouble. The girls were already suspicious, but now she somehow had to act nonchalant in front of Ryan fearing it would make him mad.

※

RYAN GLANCED at the three girls sitting at the table in the restaurant. An unwelcome air about the place as the conversation stopped and the three women stared at him, like he was public enemy number one. He hadn't called, but just dropped by to tell Taylor he was bringing barbecue brisket tonight for a late dinner. And hopefully another romp in her bed.

They had been going at sex like newlyweds. Every chance they had, they were exploring each other's bodies. He wanted to take her back out to his family's farm and shake some dust from the walls with her moans and groans. And sit outside by the fire and watch the stars together. Right now, he was desperate for some time with Taylor.

Walking over to their table, he noticed the panic in Taylor's eyes. She was trying to signal him and he knew without saying a word what she was telling him. No, the girls, her best-friends, his ex-girlfriend didn't know they were dating.

Of course, they had not made any commitments to each other, but Ryan was not one to share and when he had sex with a woman, they were exclusive. Sharing was not an option.

"Good evening, ladies," he said.

"Sheriff, what brings you by?" Taylor asked.

So many things came to mind that he realized would only upset her, so instead he lied, playing her game for now. "I wanted to tell you that I wouldn't be on duty tonight. So I won't be here to walk you home."

She nodded and rose. "That's fine. I just appreciate it when you come by. Come to the kitchen. I have something for you."

He grinned. She made his favorite desert. He was going to enjoy it with her curled by his side.

"Thank you, Taylor."

"It's the least I can do since you've been escorting me home," she said and together the two of them walked away from the table.

Out of earshot and away from prying eyes, she turned toward him. "I'm sorry, I haven't told them yet."

He grabbed her and laid a kiss on her mouth, plundering her lips with his, showing Taylor how much he wanted her. She better tell those women.

She brought her hands up between them and pushed him away. "Ryan," she said, her cheeks flushed, her mouth swollen from his kiss. Now he had branded her with his lips and she looked like she'd been appropriately kissed.

Try explaining that to the girls, he thought smiling.

"Yes," he said with a grin. "You need to tell them. You're running out of time. I'm not going to be quiet about us much longer."

Picking up the box he turned and walked out of the restaurant forgetting to tell her about the brisket.

He didn't like hiding something from view of everyone, not even his old ex who needed to get over the past. Let it go. He'd been wrong. He'd been young and he'd been stupid.

But how many years would he have to pay for that one act of foolishness? How many times would he lose someone because of his actions? People made mistakes.

CHAPTER 8

$\mathcal{T}$aylor walked in her house after a long day at the restaurant. Zeus greeted her, dancing and jumping on her while giving shrill barks telling how excited he was she came home. There was nothing like the love of a dog. Uncomplicated and sincere.

"Hi, baby," she said, setting her purse on her kitchen counter. Opening the back door, the dog ran out to do his business.

She walked back to her bedroom, kicking off her shoes when the doorbell rang. With a frown, she wondered who could be here at this time of night and knew.

Anger had her walking to the door and yanking it open.

He frowned. "You didn't check to see who it was through the peep hole."

"It was you."

Without asking him in, he walked through the door and kissed her on the lips. "Always check. It might not have been me."

"I thought you said the city of Cupid was a safe place to live?"

"It is, most of the time. Occasionally every place has issues."

Once she closed the door, he pulled her into his arms and she stiffened. Pulling back, he gazed at her, his forehead scrunched. "What's wrong?"

"Do you know how long it took me to convince them we weren't dating?"

"Maybe that's the problem. You shouldn't be trying to persuade them of what's not true. Maybe you should just tell them the truth."

Shaking her head, she stared at him. "It's not that simple."

"I need to talk to Kelsey privately and tell her about us. I didn't want to create a scene in the diner. What are we doing, Ryan, besides having sex?"

They walked into the kitchen and she let the dog back in the house. He ran over to Ryan like he just found his long, lost, best friend. Seeing Ryan made her happy, yet she'd been so angry with him for kissing her senseless and then leaving her to face the girls.

"We're developing a relationship. We're exploring each other's mind and body to find out if this thing between us is real and everlasting. And your friends should accept we're together."

Sinking down on the couch, she watched him walk over and sit beside her. "Everything is moving so fast. We went from one date to suddenly in bed and I'm afraid. We might burn out just as quickly."

"What is it going to take to calm your fears?" he asked.

She didn't want to respond to his question. At the moment, her life was peaceful. She didn't need the stress of dealing with her friends' reactions to Ryan. She was enjoying this time; why wasn't that good enough for him?

"I don't want to tell everyone we're dating and then the next day say oops, I'm sorry, we broke up. I like that we're keeping this our secret for now."

"But I hate hiding like what we're doing is wrong. I won't do it much longer, Taylor. Not for you, not for Kelsey or Meghan. If you're going to be my girl, I want everyone to know we're together."

The words were genuine and seemed to take the edge off the frustration that had been brewing between them. Yet, she still needed to talk to Kelsey. Her time was running out. Ryan wouldn't give her much longer.

Leaning into him, she felt his lips on the side of her neck. "There's something I need to tell you," he said softly, his hand curling around the curve of her breast. She lifted her chest closer to him, needing his touch.

"Later," she said, her lips moving across his chest "We've done enough talking. Show me what you really came for."

With a groan, he picked her up and carried her into the bedroom. "I'm going to make you scream my name."

She giggled. "Yes, Officer, please. Make me scream, then rescue me."

ॐ

THE MORNING RUSH was just about over when the door to the diner opened and Jack strolled in, a haggard look on his face. Picking up the coffee pot, she walked over and filled his cup. "Morning, Jack."

He glanced up her. "You're certainly chipper this morning. You and that new boyfriend doing all right?"

"Yes," she said, remembering last night and how many times she'd climaxed before falling asleep in his arms. A deep, sound sleep until the alarm alerted her it was time to leave him with her dog cuddling in bed while she went to work.

That had been hard. Damn hard.

"What time does your family arrive."

He sighed and watched as the waitress delivered his eggs. "Trip was called off. The granddaughter has some kind of band activity, and well, my daughter said they would come this summer. We'll see."

"When was the last time you saw them?" she asked.

"Margaret's funeral," he said, taking a bite of his toast. "No reason to come visit the old man anymore."

"Don't say that, Jack," she said, upset at the very idea. "They're just busy. Your granddaughter's at that age where friends and school take over. You think your grandparents will always be there."

As he picked up his coffee cup, she noticed a tremor in his hands. "Margaret's gone and I don't know how much longer I'll be around. I'm not as young as I use to be."

His words left her anxious, but yet, he wasn't that old. Nowadays, being in your sixties was young.

"You're going to be coming in here and checking on me. You have to make certain this new man sticks around."

He gave a half-hearted smile. "You always brighten my day. I could eat breakfast at home, but I enjoy your company."

"I enjoy yours as well."

He pushed his plate away. "Did you tell your friends about this man?"

She chewed her lip. "No. I hate to cause a ruckus. We've only been back in town together a little more than a month. What if this doesn't work out between me and Ryan? What if next week he's off chasing some other woman? I could be his first pass through the buffet line."

Jack started laughing. "A good thing you're in the restaurant business. You can connect anything in life to food."

Taylor smiled. "Well, I had a knowledgeable teacher. My mother connected desserts to all life lessons."

He lifted his coffee mug to his lips and gazed at her. "A good man doesn't go through the buffet line once or twice before he finds something that interests him. If your man is as smart as I think he is, he'll know he's found a dish that is going to satisfy him for a long time. Someone who will stand by him, support him, and even give him little pumpkin pies - my personal favorite."

"Jack, you make everything in life sound so easy. Are you saying take a breath and give it time."

"I am."

She kept reminding herself to relax and have fun with Ryan. Eventually everything would work out. Time was running out and soon she knew he would force her to tell the world about their relationship.

"What if I find out something horrible about him? What if I learn he's doing something terrible?"

"What is your gut instinct telling you?"

"Relax. He's a wonderful man. Even better than my disastrous fiancé."

"There you go," Jack said. "Quit worrying about the future and appreciate the here and now."

Sighing, Taylor noticed the dark circles under Jack's eyes. "You all right?"

"Been a bit tired the last few days. I'm getting old. Whatever it is, it's not a big deal."

"I still think I need to set you up with an online matchmaking site. You might find someone else."

He smiled. "Oh no. I had a great married life, a lovely wife and lover. I don't want to take a chance and ruin my record."

"I want a marriage like you had with Margaret. After I'm gone, I want my man to miss me like you miss your wife. I want him to say I was a great companion."

He smiled. "All it takes is complete honesty, treat your husband right and shower him with love. It's simple and yet hard. There were days when nothing went right, the kids, job issues, money problems. But in the end, I would do it all over again."

She grinned. "Did Margaret ever dance around the Cupid statue?"

He laughed. "No. But she threw a coin in the fountain and made a wish the day before I asked her to marry me."

"Oh no! I'm in so much trouble," she said, her chest freezing. Could her and Ryan be meant to be together.

"Why?"

"That's where I became reacquainted with the man I'm dating."

He stood and she did as well. He gave her hug. "Remember, if your love is meant to be, it will come easy. Always keep that in mind. Have a great day."

"You, too, Jack," she said and watched him walk out the door.

The man was sad, yet she also enjoyed talking to him

Her eyes widened at the thought and she looked out the window to watch him walk toward his truck. Such a lonely man and yet he'd experienced the greatest treasures life had to offer with his lovely wife, Margaret.

৯.

THE NEXT MORNING, Jack didn't show up for breakfast. At first, she worried when she realized he hadn't come in, but she remembered her mother saying sometimes he came in for supper. He didn't come in. On the second morning he didn't come in, she looked up his phone number and called. No answer, just his wife's lovely voice on the message machine.

She considered calling Ryan and having him drive out to her friend's place, but didn't want to appear an alarmist. Later that day Ryan came into the restaurant and sat in her office. "What time are you coming home tonight?"

Her brows crinkled together. "Around the same time as every night."

"I thought maybe you could leave a little early. We'd go out to the ranch and make sure the cattle are all right, watch the stars and melt a few s'mores."

She laughed. "I'd love to, but my cook called in sick today and two deliveries arrived to shelve. You can always come here and restock my shelves."

"And have to hide in the back in case your girlfriends come in? I don't think so," he said. "I bought some new lotion that guarantees pleasure for each partner." He grinned. "I thought later you could rub some on my back."

Leaning back in her chair, she gazed at him. "Why do I have the feeling this cream you want on your back, you also want on your front?"

"You're such a quick learner. I'm so impressed," he said, laughing as he stood.

"Common male psychology," she replied. "Always in need of a lube job."

"Thank you," he said. Bending over the desk, he leaned close to her and whispered, "I thought you liked my lube job."

"Very much," she said softly, kissing him on the lips. Everything came easy with Ryan. Somehow they'd fallen into a pattern of him showing up at her door every night. Many times, staying over. It felt comfortable. Right. "See you at the house tonight."

"Later," he said and walked out the door.

Jumping up she ran after him. "Wait. Ryan, I need a favor."

"What?" he questioned.

"Jack Larkin has not been in the diner for the last two days. He comes in every day. I tried to call him, but no one answers. I'm sure he's okay, but would you please go out to his place and check on him. I'm concerned."

"Sure," he said. "I know he lives out on Glassier Road. I'm sure it's nothing, but I'll swing out there to make sure."

"Thanks," she said smiling and blew him a kiss as she watched him leave.

CHAPTER 9

*R*yan pulled up in front of Taylor's home in his patrol car. He should have gone home first, but he couldn't. In law enforcement, there were days you questioned why you did this job. Today was one of those days.

Numb from the afternoon events, he walked up to the door and rang the bell. He didn't care his car sat parked on the street for anyone to see if they drove by, including her girlfriends. Taylor needed to accept the time to acknowledge they were dating had come. No more hiding.

And after today, he longed for the sanctity of her arms around him when he gave her the bad news.

She opened the door. "Hey, I was about to give up on you."

Coming inside, she gazed at him suspiciously. "You haven't been home?" Glancing outside she frowned. "You're still in your patrol car."

Staring at her, he watched the slow comprehension on her face that something was wrong, terribly wrong.

"What happened?" she asked. "A bad car wreck on the highway?"

The tenseness in his body gave him away, but the realization of what occurred still hadn't connected for Taylor. He hated the news about Jack.

"It's Jack," he said slowly.

"Is he sick?" she asked, her eyes widening in fright. "Is he in the hospital? Please tell me he's all right," she said her voice rising.

Shaking his head, he went to her and wrapped his arms around her. "Doc said it looks like he suffered a massive heart attack. He died before he could call 911."

"No," she cried. "No. No. Tell me he didn't die alone."

"I went there after we spoke," Ryan said, feeling numb inside. "He sat in his chair."

The memory of Jack sitting there looking so peaceful would never leave Ryan. From the window, he seemed fine, but he never moved and never would again.

"The doc came out, pronounced him dead. Then I waited for the coroner. Contacted his daughter and..." he ran his hand through his hair. "Tonight has been a really long night."

Taylor began to cry. "He's been so depressed about his wife. Being all by himself in that big house, I knew he was lonely. But this..."

Tears rolled down her cheeks and Ryan saw the shock and numbness wearing off, giving over to grief. "We became such good friends."

"I know," he said, holding her while she sobbed against his shoulder.

When someone perished alone, it becomes a lawman's worst nightmare. Especially calling their next of kin and telling them over the phone or in person. You tried to say things that would make that person feel better, yet what can you say that will ease their grief.

"Coroner said he went quickly. I found him sitting in his chair, the television still blaring," he said, his voice cracking.

Just the act of breaking into a person's house when they didn't answer the door bell was disturbing. Ryan spoke often with the man and the sight of him dead ripped at his insides leaving an empty hollow. Death was never pretty.

"Thank goodness you asked me to check on him," he said, thinking the more time elapsed before they found his body, it would have been worse.

"He's with his wife," Taylor said crying. "I'll miss him so much, but he's happy to be with her. He's no longer alone."

Ryan didn't know or care who was more upset. Him because of the gruesome discovery or Taylor because she'd lost her friend.

"Let's sit down," he said. He'd been on his feet for almost eight hours since finding the body. Spent, both emotionally and physically, Ryan needed some time away from his job in the arms of Taylor.

Sinking to her couch, she curled into his chest. "Are you all right?"

What could he say? He'd done his duty and yet this part of law enforcement he detested. "Worried about you. You were friends."

"He educated me about men and women better than anyone, including my parents. He and his wife, they lived a wonderful life together and he explained to me what you need in a loving marriage."

Jack had been an acquaintance. A nice man, who frequented town and supported the sheriff's department. Taylor had been closer to him than Ryan. Often she spoke of him with a wistful tone. "Tell me what he taught you."

"We talked about so many things. The biggest thing he shared was simple. If a relationship doesn't come easy, then it's probably not going to last."

Stunned Ryan stared at her. He'd never thought about dating that way before. It made sense. How many times had he gone out with women where everything became a battle. Yet with Taylor, their time together had been easy going, effortless, and oh, so enjoyable.

She gave a sad sigh. "He made me realize how fortunate I'd not married a man who cheated on me."

Ryan cringed.

She laughed through her tears. "He told me stories about him and Margaret and how their marriage worked. Their life wasn't all sunshine and roses. They dealt with real life issues, but they stuck it out together even when they disagreed."

Life gave everyone problems, but when you found the right partner, he could see how it would make life easier.

"He said every couple has times of good and bad. He helped me understand when your companion comes along, we'll learn to work out our differences and always put the relationship first because we love each other."

She cried harder against his shoulder.

Warmth spread through him as he clung to Taylor like an anchor in life's storms. In the short time they'd been with each other, being with her had been smooth except for the hiding. Which had to stop. Together they needed to face his past transgressions.

Ryan thought about what the old gentleman had taught Taylor and how it applied to the two of them. A warm aching need filled him as he held the woman he realized he was rapidly falling in love with.

When he awoke in the morning his thoughts were of Taylor and the last person he pictured as he closed his eyes was the woman sitting beside him. He couldn't wait to gaze into her blue eyes, laugh with her, be with her, hold her. He wanted to spend forever with Taylor.

Every night he wanted to come home after a difficult day to Taylor. Making her smile, being with her and that silly mutt she called a dog, and waking up in her arms every morning--he wanted that every day.

If they were going to work out their conflicts, he needed to confess. Tomorrow he would tell her his secret. Soon he would admit only she could capture his heart and that he'd made a terrible mistake with Kelsey and even Taylor by lying. In the beginning, if he'd been honest, she would never have given them a chance. Now he knew he loved her and she deserved to be told the truth.

Ryan wanted her in his life every day. Jack had helped him and Taylor and now the old guy had departed for the next life before he had the opportunity to tell him thank you.

"You're going to miss Jack," he said kissing her neck.

"Yes," she whispered. "I ache so badly for his daughter. She planned to come visit him this summer." She snuggled closer to him. "Talking to him every day over breakfast, he taught me so much."

"And that's what you should always remember about him," he said, trailing kisses along her neck, her jaw, moving to her lips.

Covering her mouth with his, he drank of her lips, his tongue seeking out and dancing with her own. The thought of losing her, caused his chest to ache, his heart pounding. He loved Taylor. He wanted her in his life for more than just a day or a night or a flashing moment. He wanted a home, babies, and to grow old together.

Would she have him once she learned he cheated?

Breaking the kiss, she gazed into his eyes, her blue eyes filled with longing.

"Come to bed, Ryan," she said. "I need you."

She didn't have to ask him twice.

TAYLOR LED Ryan into the bedroom. Tonight, she needed him to chase away the darkness and make her feel like she could find love. A love like Jack and his wife. A connection that would bind her to someone, hopefully Ryan, forever.

She knew she was falling in love with him. For weeks, she

denied her growing feelings because she feared getting hurt again. Afraid of the commitment to yet another man who worked in a profession brimming with danger and recklessness and a disregard for monogamy. Yet, Ryan had been faithful to her and displayed more of the goodness of a lawman. He rescued cats, he kept the peace, he helped the elderly and even the deceased.

There was so much more to this man that she loved, and though she didn't want to cause Kelsey pain, she had a chance at happiness that she wasn't willing to walk away from. Tomorrow she would speak with her friend and tell her the truth.

Pulling Ryan through the door, she began to remove his uniform. His fingers came up to help her and she pushed them away.

"Let me," she said. The night had been traumatic for both. Finding her friend dead had been difficult for Ryan and she sought comfort in his arms. Together they would find solace and life affirming, healing love.

Yes, she mourned Jack's death, but realized he was at peace. No longer missing the woman who walked beside him on earth. With one another again, only those left behind suffered their loss. Including her.

Unbuttoning Ryan's shirt, she pulled the garment from his pants and tossed it on to the chair. Then she went to work unbuckling his belt.

"I'll unhook my holster," he said, taking the gun and laying it on her dresser.

Pushing him down on the bed, she removed his boots, his socks and then pulled him to stand. Her fingers returned to the hook on his jeans. With a swish they landed on the floor, where he stepped from them. When she reached up and hooked her hand in his underwear and yanked them down, his penis popped out, jutting proudly in front of him, hard and dangerous looking.

Touching the tip, she glanced at him and he pulled her into his arms.

"Ryan," she whispered as she pulled her top over her head and then stared at him in the darkened room. "Make love to me."

She knew it would be love. Her heart swelled as tears filled her eyes. She wasn't crying for Jack or even for herself. These tears were joyful tears. This man helped her realize love was about sacrifice and giving of one's self for the other. And he'd done that on more than one occasion.

His mouth covered hers, dragging her naked body closer. His kiss demanded her surrender, and she eagerly complied. She'd give him her heart, her soul, her body, and knew he would protect and love her. They hadn't said the words yet, but their actions showed the emotion.

Falling to the bed, he took her with him. Her body hummed with a pulsing heat the friction of his skin against hers generated. His hands caressed her breasts as he kissed her, and her pulse pounded with a rhythm he created.

A moan escaped as his fingers skimmed down her flesh, leaving a trail of molten fire that had her gasping for breath.

"Ryan," she said as his digits delved through her silken folds, his lips suckling, pulling at her nipples, sending shivers of need through her.

Why did this man seem to be the only one who connected with her in such a sensual way that they seemed in tune, their bodies knowing what the other demanded?

Grabbing his rod, she stroked the length, her hand caressing the end, spreading the moisture she found there. His loving touch created a firestorm of sensations like a hurricane of heat rushing at her. Her body clamored for the fill of him. Her need roaring within her.

"Now," she said. "Take me now."

"Gladly," he replied as he shoved his penis into her slickened folds.

Together they rode the crest, the two of them merging and melting with each stroke as she stared up into his brown eyes, losing herself in his gaze. There was no other man she wanted to spend the rest of her days alongside. With Ryan, she wanted to have babies, grow old, and even die together.

Love pulsed through her veins, flowing from her eyes and into his heart as they came together with a final shudder and a gasp. Reaffirming life and love, they clung to one another, their breath slowing, their hearts beating simultaneously.

Taylor felt gratitude that love found her right here in her home town.

❧

RYAN HELD her love in his hands and yet her best friend had suffered heart break because of him. Before she told Ryan she loved him, before she committed herself to him, she needed to understand why Kelsey hated the sheriff.

She invited Kelsey for breakfast at the house this morning, where they could talk in private. Taylor felt an urgency to know what happened between her and Ryan.

Enjoying being with Ryan and fearful of what Kelsey would tell her, Taylor had resisted this conversation way too long.

The doorbell rang and a nervous tremor shuddered through her. Should she tell Kelsey she was sleeping with Ryan. Last night in his arms, they'd found solace, comforting each other from the painful reminder of how life could be snatched away in a second. Ryan had been honest and sincere and now she would break the news to Kelsey that she loved the sheriff.

As she opened the door, Zeus went crazy barking at her friend, while she hugged her. "I fixed coffee and your favorite Snickerdoodles are in the oven. I thought we could dip cookies in our coffee."

"If today was a lazy day, we should add some Irish cream to our brew. I'm working on the shop and the boys are coming to help me in two hours."

"Come into the kitchen," Taylor said. "Ignore the dog. He'll soon be licking your hand. Especially if you offer him food."

They walked into the warm, cozy room and she poured them a cup of the coffee. Taking the cookies out of the oven, they grabbed a few of the sweets and sat at the table.

"You message sounded urgent. What's going on?" Kelsey asked with Zeus demanding attention at her feet, begging for a scrap.

Taylor took a deep breath. "I need to ask you something. You can tell me it's none of my business if you choose, but I want you to tell me your side of what happened between you and Ryan."

Kelsey shook her head and frowned. "Are you dating him?"

Taylor wanted to hear what Kelsey said before she admitted her relationship with the sheriff. "What went wrong between the two of you."

With a shake of her dark hair, Kelsey tilted her head and sighed. "Ryan was my first serious boyfriend. We were young, and I thought, in love. But I was living in the fairy dust land. I had dreams of flowers and lace and happily ever after. My family didn't like him, but I would have followed him to the ends of the earth. Then I found out he cheated on me."

"What?" Taylor said, her heart stopping as her stomach clenched. Nausea roiled through her like a thunderstorm. Ryan cheated on Kelsey. He lied.

"Who was he with?" she asked stunned, reeling from the anguish of his deception. He'd promised Taylor he'd never been unfaithful. Never. How stupid could he be? Didn't he think she would find out the truth. Kelsey was one of her oldest and dearest friends. What the hell was wrong with this man? He even encouraged her to talk to Kelsey.

"He had sex with Rhonda Smothers. That tramp who went to all those parties the boys held."

Taylor thought about the girl, who in high school, was known as easy and suddenly doubt filled her. Her Ryan would never condone that type of behavior. "Are you certain?"

"Of course," she said. "He confessed."

Taylor sat there absorbing the news. At that time in their life, they were all so young and naive, yet believed school had made them ready to tackle the world. They thought they knew everything when they hadn't received the first vowel.

"It happened at the last graduation party. The one held out at the lake. My parents said I couldn't attend because my brothers told them there would be alcohol. Ryan attended while I went shopping with my mother," she said shaking her head. "We should have broken up before the end of school. And probably would have if my brothers had minded their own business and not insisted I stop seeing him. Instead, I held on, knowing being with Ryan drove my family crazy."

"Is this why you left town so suddenly?"

She nodded. "After the party, I didn't hear from him for three days. Then I ran into Rhonda. She grinned and proceeded to tell me all about her new studly boyfriend, Ryan. She was cruel in how bluntly she told me about having sex with him and how I should have put out."

"What a bitch," Taylor said, remembering the agony of Kevin being unfaithful. Those awful feelings of hurt and disillusionment that left her leery of men. How could she trust a man who thought nothing about lying to her about how he'd hurt her friend?

"Yes, she was. When I got home, I called Ryan and asked him if I'd been replaced. He came rushing over. Outside in front of my house, he confessed he drank too much that night and got drunk. The next thing he knew he and Rhonda were having sex. He felt bad, but I couldn't forgive him.

"My brothers looked out the window, saw me crying and screaming at him and they came storming out. The fight was on."

Kelsey shook her head and took a sip of the hot drink. "Before I realized what was happening, my brother Jim was beating the crap out of him. One of the neighbors called the sheriff to come break up a brawl. My mother came out of the house and hauled me inside while my father calmed everyone down and kept them from going to jail."

What else was Ryan hiding from her? How had he forgotten to mention this little incident and did he really think she would never find out? What kind of man deliberately thought he could get away with lying?

"Afterwards, my family thought best if I spent the summer traveling abroad before going off to college. I should tell him thank you for giving me a wonderful travel experience, but I grieved for weeks after I learned he slept with Rhonda."

Taylor bit her lip. The question hovering in her mind that she didn't want to ask, but needed to know. "Do you still care for him?"

Her friend shrugged like it no longer mattered, but Taylor didn't believe her.

"Our breakup was for the best. I don't begrudge him any longer. I'm not pining away yearning for him. There are no lingering feelings. A nicer, non-threatening law enforcement involved ending would have mended our fences years ago. Hey, I got a trip to Europe because of him."

She stared at Taylor and gave her the evil stink eye. "Are you certain the two of you are not an item?"

How could Taylor answer Kelsey's question without hurting her even more? She'd fallen in love with the man only to learn he was creative with the truth. After he promised her he never cheated and she accepted his word, then finding out he two-timed Kelsey... When would he be unfaithful to Taylor? "No. Not anymore."

Kelsey gazed at her like she didn't quite believe Taylor.

"But you were seeing Ryan?"

Unable to glance at her friend, she sighed. "We went out a couple of times," she admitted.

She was not about to tell her the last few weeks the two of

them had been burning up the sheets together. Not now when the pain of his betrayal ached like a surgeon carved her heart out without anesthesia. Bitterness filled her throat almost gagging her and she longed to curl up in a ball and cry. God, how she missed Jack. He understood men and helped her comprehend the reasons behind their behavior.

"Look, I care about you, Taylor. You're my friend. Maybe he's changed. I don't want him to hurt you like he did me. You said it yourself that you like lawmen and they cheat. He's got a proven record of not being faithful. Don't let him sweet talk you into believing he's a good guy."

Sighing, Taylor glanced at Kelsey. Everything she said about Ryan was true. Everything she said about Taylor was true. She couldn't deny being a sucker for a man in a uniform wearing a gun. Unfortunately, they liked to live dangerously.

"I know. I just wanted to make certain I heard your side of the story. We're not dating," she said, knowing she would end it with Ryan. Stick a fork in her, they were done.

At this point it wasn't even the fact he had been traitorous. It was more about the lie he told. He knowingly misguided Taylor. Now Taylor appeared dumb. Ignorant for thinking he was different. For believing him when he said he never cheated.

CHAPTER 10

*R*yan was ready for this day to be over. First, he'd given one of his officers a formal reprimand when he caught him hitting a prisoner. The mouthy drug offender yelled obnoxious and offensive words at his officer, but as a lawman, you ignored the insults and did your job. Daniel let the man antagonize him and Ryan removed him immediately from the scene.

He wasn't a bad employee, but sometimes prisoners got under your skin. When he'd called Daniel's mother a horrible name, the jailer broke and retaliated.

Later, he'd been on duty at Jack's funeral and escorted the family to the cemetery, where they laid him to rest. Ryan wanted to be with Taylor during this difficult time, and instead watched her in the distance while he stood at attention.

Sometimes the job interfered, and yet in a small town, he had a limited number of men and women on his team. Today, he couldn't attend Jack's burial as a friend, but was there in an official capacity. He hoped Taylor understood.

Finally, on his way home tonight, Mrs. Raffsberger called. Once again he dropped everything for a feline pursuit. That damn cat would be the death of him. But the little old lady only had her pets and the joy on her face when he brought the animal to her warmed his heart. And she always gave him a pie or cake to take to the station to share with everyone.

Maybe he was nothing but an oversized lump of mush, but how could he refuse to help her? Alone at eighty-three, there was no one left to chase her cats but Ryan.

In front of the restaurant, he noticed all the lights were out. He glanced at his watch and realized at ten minutes after nine, she'd closed-up and gone home already.

As he drove the route she walked home, he searched until he arrived at her house. He couldn't have missed her by much. A warm glow came from inside and he could hear Zeus barking.

Knocking on the door, he heard the dog yapping excitedly. The door opened and there she stood. Every time he saw her, a rush of excitement went through him.

"Hi," she said.

Sadness gazed from her red-rimmed eyes where she'd been crying. "Tough day?"

"Yes," she said and he walked through the door. He gave her a quick kiss on the lips, knowing he couldn't wait to take her in his arms.

Reaching down, he petted Zeus who jumped and danced around like his best friend just walked in.

"I saw you at the funeral, but when I finally got free, you were gone," he said.

"I spoke to his daughter and then I left," she said. "He's no longer there."

"No," he said knowing she was right, but shocked she didn't wait for him.

They sank down on the couch at the same time. She turned to face him, bringing up a leg to keep him from getting closer. He frowned. Usually they sat holding one another for at least ten to twenty minutes, just talking. Tonight, she seemed to be trembling in her corner, keeping distance between them. What was wrong?

"You and the girls still going to the spa this weekend?" he asked.

"Yes," she said. "We're leaving day after tomorrow."

It would be lonely without her, but then this week he was working every day but Sunday.

"Kelsey came over this morning," she said.

A trickle of alarm spiraled up his spine. For days, he meant to tell her before they left for their retreat, knowing she needed to know before the women were all together about his reasons for lying.

"I asked her to have breakfast with me so I could understand why the two of you haven't patched things up. I couldn't fathom how a break-up in high school would leave two people hating each other as much as you two obviously do."

"I don't hate Kelsey," he said wanting her to know right up front that he held no animosity toward the woman he'd done wrong.

"She told me what happened between the two of you," Taylor said, her voice stern, her eyes wide and her hands shaking. "You lied. You said you'd never cheated. Yet you cheated on Kelsey."

How could he make this better? He was in so much trouble. He faced her, trying to think of any way to get out of this, realizing he'd been caught. "You're right. I lied to you. I wanted to spend time with you, get to know you and show you not all lawmen are cheaters. I knew if I told you the truth, you would never go out with me."

"Why didn't you tell me before I found out?" she asked.

"I tried. Every time I went to tell you, something would happen. I put off being honest with you because I knew this would not be an easy conversation."

"No, it's not," Taylor said.

"Look, I did two-time Kelsey, but I would never do that to

you. At eighteen, I was a young, stupid, horny male who wanted to experience sex. A virgin who wanted to prove I was a man. I got drunk that night and later learned I screwed Rhonda. I don't even remember being with her. After seeing how much my indiscretion hurt Kelsey, I swore to never cheat on another woman. And I haven't."

"But you deceived me."

"I had no choice if I wanted to spend time with you. I don't regret this time together. I crave being with you, only you. No one else."

She turned her blue eyes on him. They were glistening with tears. "I was falling for you. I thought that whatever this thing is between us could grow into forever. How can I build trust with a man who lies? How can I ever be certain you're telling me the truth?"

He swallowed, his chest aching with the pain. How could he argue with her? She was right, but he hadn't duped her in a mean spirited way. His reasoning had been selfish. But his stupid high school drunken mistake was not something he told everyone.

Running his hand through his hair, he sighed. "I'm so damn honest, it hurts. But you're right. I mislead you about Kelsey because I wanted no one else but you."

A tear trickled down her cheek. "I think you should go. I need some time to think."

"Taylor," he said, fearing that if he left, she would never let him back in. "Everyone makes mistakes. I made a huge one when I stepped out on Kelsey. I was wrong and I'm sorry. When I deliberately deceived you, I did it because I wanted to be with you. There are no doubts in my mind. I still want to be with you."

She shook her head. "You've got to go."

He rose, feeling like a fifty pound weight sat on his chest. He loved her. He hadn't told her because he wanted the moment to be special and everlasting. And now it appeared that moment would never come.

"I'm leaving, Taylor, but I'm not giving up on us. I want to be with you," he said walking to the door.

She didn't say anything, but turned her back as he left her townhome.

❧

FOR TWO DAYS, Ryan couldn't sleep. He couldn't eat and it was a good thing the Raffsberger's cat didn't come up missing or he might've jail that pussy. He worked, he moped and grew angrier.

An incident in his life at the age of eighteen still wreaked havoc on his life. He missed Taylor's closeness, the smell of her, her smile, and the way she would take his hand in hers and squeeze their palms together.

She was his missing half and he wanted her back. For two days, he gave her space, knowing she needed time and distance to realize the worst crime he committed against her was wanting to be with her.

At night, he followed in the patrol car not far from her, watching her walk home, tormenting himself because he couldn't chase her down, pull her in his arms and kiss her senseless.

He loved her and needed her.

His mind searched frantically for some solution that would make her grasp his lie showed he cared. Tomorrow, she was going to the spa to be with her girlfriends. She'd be with Meghan and Kelsey.

Like a slap to the face, the solution hit him and he groaned. The idea was perfect, but gut wrenching. Grabbing his hat, he slipped on his coat and strolled out the door.

Five minutes later, he pulled up in front of the Kelsey's Boutique, where he hoped to find Kelsey inside.

Opening the door, he heard her working.

"Cody, is that you? I'm almost ready," she called.

113

"No, it's Ryan," he said, his strides taking him toward her voice.

She came around the corner and stared at him. "What are you doing here?"

He removed his hat and twirled it nervously in his hand. "I know you hate my guts and I can't blame you."

"I don't hate your guts," she said frowning.

"Well, let's just say I came here today to apologize. At the time, I was an eighteen-year-old horny boy who was disappointed when I couldn't get into your pants."

She laughed.

"At the graduation party, after several shots of tequila, the alcohol loosened me up and made me stupid. I started making out with Rhonda which led me to cheating on you." Hanging his head for a moment, he looked into her eyes. "I want to say how sorry I am. If I had remained sober, the teenage hormones would never have gotten loose."

He glanced into her eyes and noticed they sparkled with what appeared to be laughter. How she must enjoy hearing him grovel after all these years.

"That night taught me a very valuable lesson. Never drink until I lose control. Besides the tequila making me sick, I could have caught any number of diseases or created a baby with a woman I didn't even like. Young and stupid, I just wanted to experience sex for the first time. Cheating on you exposed the damage I could cause. I've never stepped out on another girl. Please forgive me."

Kelsey smiled. "We were childish and naive," she said. "I must thank you. Because of you, I got a tour of Europe that summer. Mom and Dad wanted to keep us apart so we took off traveling. It was the best trip of my life."

"I'm glad something good came out of it for you," he said. "Your brothers beat the crap out of me that day."

"Sorry. They've always been awfully protective of me. Sometimes a little overly protective. What made you come over here today and tell me this? Is it because of my meeting with Taylor?"

He bit the inside of his mouth, scrunching his eyes shut and then opened them wide before he spoke. "We're taking some time. She's kept everyone in the dark about us seeing each other, but I really care about her, Kelsey. We have fun together. We fit each other, but more than anything, she makes me happy."

Nodding, Kelsey laughed. "What are you going to do?" she asked.

"I'm lost. I want her back in my life. Yes, I lied, but I did because I wanted to be with Taylor. Something drew me to her and I had to know if there was a possibility of this attraction growing. She would never have given us the chance. Now, I want to ask her to marry me, have children with her, grow old together," he said.

Kelsey frowned. "I can't believe I'm saying this." She shook her head and gave a little snort. "Give me some time. We'll all be together at the spa on Saturday. Let me see if I can somehow help her understand."

He wanted to grab and hug her, but refrained. That was not how you proved to your ex-girlfriend you were being loyal to your current girl.

"I would so appreciate any help you can give me. Thank you," he said, standing there awkwardly, he glanced around the store. "Your shop looks nice."

"Thanks. Now get out of here before my boyfriend arrives and finds us together. I don't want a repeat of our teenage years. What a crazy day."

"Your brothers let you have a boyfriend?" he asked his brows raising.

"Yes. My brothers don't know yet."

He shook his head. "I pity the poor man. Tell him that Jim has a mean right hook."

"I'll warn him," she said and walked him out the door.

"Thanks for coming by and apologizing. Let's put the past behind us and start fresh," she said.

So grateful, he gave her a polite, gentlemanly squeeze. "Agreed. Enjoy the spa."

"Oh, we will," she said smiling as she closed the door behind him.

Ryan had done everything he could to save his relationship. Soon it would be in Taylor's hands as to whether or not they stayed together.

TAYLOR GLANCED AROUND at her friends as they sat in their bathrobes with their hair up in towels, drinking a glass of wine while they received a pedicure. They'd already gotten a massage and a facial. So far the day had been fun. Tonight, they had reservations at an expensive restaurant and were staying at an exclusive hotel in downtown Dallas.

Meghan laid back in the chair with her eyes closed. "This is the life. We should plan on doing this at least once a quarter."

"Maybe," Kelsey said watching the young man wrap her legs in a towel. "Depends on how the shop does."

"If I can find someone to cover the diner, I'm game," Taylor said.

Kelsey sighed. "I have a confession to make."

Taylor gazed at her friend an uneasy sense overcoming her. What would Kelsey share?

"Ryan came to see me yesterday. After almost seven years, we finally put to bed the past. He apologized about how he hurt me."

"What?" Meghan said. "I knew you guys broke up, but what did he do."

"He cheated," Taylor said. "An apology doesn't make it right."

"He had some excellent points. He admitted to being a young, horny boy who just wanted to get into any girl's pants. And when you add tequila and a willing teenage girl to a high school party, you get trouble."

"Still doesn't excuse what he did," Taylor said.

"Hmmm," Meghan replied. "Did you ever have too much to drink in college and do something stupid?"

Taylor frowned. But that didn't compare, did it? Looking back, her college days were filled with high jinks that left her less than perfect. In fact, she was lucky to live to tell about some of her escapades. Ryan pulled his stupid stunt in high school. She no longer did those wild and crazy stunts. What made him exempt from evolving into a better person?

"I certainly did. It was a wonder I graduated," Taylor said, not liking the direction of this conversation.

"I told you how I popped my cherry in college. No, I'm not proud. What makes me any different from Ryan?" Kelsey asked.

Sitting there, Taylor didn't say a word, but listened as the two girls talked. Meghan didn't know about her dating Ryan, and Kelsey wondered if she realized how serious Taylor and Ryan were before she discovered his deceit.

"Did he do this to convince you to talk me into going out with him again?"

Kelsey laughed. "No, we didn't discuss you much. Though for only being on one date, the man seemed pretty crazy about you. You kept us in the dark regarding you and Ryan."

She swallowed. Well, rats. He told Kelsey about the two of them being together.

Meghan sat up, her eyes widening with surprise. "You and Ryan? Seeing one another? Really?"

She started laughing and sunk back on the chair.

"Yes, me and Ryan," Taylor said, wishing she'd been honest with them. "But he lied to me."

"What person hasn't told a fib to make themselves look better," Kelsey said. "You've never distorted or misrepresented something? Never kept anything from your friends?"

Well, crap, this just kept getting better and better. Yes, she hadn't been truthful to them about her and Ryan. "Okay, so I didn't tell you the truth about Ryan."

Meghan snickered softly.

"Do you love him?" Kelsey asked.

Tears welled up in Taylors eyes and filled her throat. This week had been horrible. Probably the worst of her life. First Jack and then the break-up with Ryan. Today on what was supposed to be a relaxing time, like a dog with a bone, Kelsey was determined to make it tough. Taylor needed some peace and tranquility. Not being forced to deal with loving a man whose morals she questioned.

"Yes, I love Ryan," she said almost shouting the words.

Kelsey smiled. "Good."

"Are you happy now?" Taylor asked.

"Why are you letting an incident that happened almost seven years ago stop you from getting the love you deserve? Why would you let the mistakes between us keep you from happiness?" Kelsey said, her voice rising with disbelief.

Taylor thought for a moment, wondering to herself why she would pass on a chance at everything she's been searching for with a man. Yet, he'd lied and cheated. Her honest lawman had done wrong.

"He had sex with someone else while the two of you dated," Taylor said vehemently. "I vowed never to date another man who can't be faithful. Ryan wasn't loyal."

Kelsey smiled that knowing grin that made Taylor nervous. "At eighteen, he wanted to lose his virginity. I wanted to surrender mine in college. Now, if he did that today, then yes, I'd be getting a rope and we'd be stringing him up in the Cupid courtyard in the town square. He wasn't the only one who screwed up. You hid this relationship from us."

"Only to protect you. You've said how much you dislike him," Taylor said.

"And I did. Yesterday, we buried the hatchet. Life is too short and he said he was sorry. How many men apologize and admit their error," Kelsey said, gazing at her friend. She picked up Taylor's hand. "You admitted you love him. Give him a break. Give him some time."

Meghan giggled even louder.

Taylor stared at her friend's polished fingernails. Kelsey was giving Ryan a second chance and would even be friends with him once again; why couldn't she?

The last few days had been the most miserable of her life. She missed Jack, but more importantly she felt like part of her was missing. Without Ryan, her life seemed empty.

"All right, I'll give him another opportunity, but I'm going to lay down some rules. This will only happen on my terms."

"Great," Kelsey said and jumped out of the foot spa much to the technician's dismay as she splashed water all over the floor in her exuberance to reach out and embrace Taylor. Meghan bounced up, giggling, splashing water everywhere and joined in the group hug.

She continued to giggle.

"Why have you laughed this entire time?" Taylor demanded.

"Don't you see," Meghan said smiling. "The Cupid superstition is finding us love. You're the first one to succumb to the spell."

"I didn't want love," Taylor said amazed at what Meghan said. Could it be real? Was the Cupid superstition working to bring her and Ryan together.

Kelsey started jumping up and down, forcing the others to follow her lead. "I have such a great idea. I know how to get you your happily ever after. I can't wait for us to return to Cupid."

Taylor smiled at her friends, certain they were all thinking the same thing.

❦

RYAN SAT IN HIS OFFICE, finishing up paperwork before he headed out. His shift was almost over and tonight he just wanted to go home, crawl in bed, and try to get some elusive rest. The last week had been difficult. Right up there with his introduction to Afghanistan and learning to adjust to a new life.

Since Taylor asked for some time, he'd been trying to adapt to living without the woman he'd fallen in love with. And he didn't like it one bit, but he would go on.

His dispatcher walked into the office and frowned. "We got some women doing the Stupid Cupid caper again. Just received a report of a naked woman dancing around the fountain in the square."

"Damn," Ryan said grabbing his coat. "I'm not in the mood for this shit. Prepare a jail cell for them. I'm tired of this crap."

All he could think about was Taylor and her friends sprinting around the statue naked. But mainly Taylor. Her firm breasts, trim waist, and legs that were long enough to curl around a man and squeeze him into forever.

The man smiled. "Go get them, Sheriff."

Keys in hand, he walked out the door. It would take him fewer than five minutes to arrive and five minutes to arrest this public nuisance, but now he didn't care. Hitting the lights, he gunned the car, racing down the street. He really needed to convince the city council to tear down Cupid.

Pulling into the square, he saw her. She wasn't naked. She sat by the fountain, waiting for him. Had Taylor made the call?

Getting out of his patrol vehicle, he glanced around and didn't see any nude women.

Stepping up in front of her, he stopped.

"Evening, Sheriff," she said.

"What are you doing, Taylor?" he asked.

"I went to the spa this weekend and spent time with the girls. Kelsey told me what you did," she gazed up at him reached out, took his hand and pulled him down beside her. The wind coming off the fountain's spray was cool and occasionally she felt a drop of moisture land on her.

He didn't say anything. He was too afraid to respond and somehow ruin what he hoped was happening.

"In the last month, I've fallen in love with you, grown to know you and how you care for the people in this community. How you chase Mrs. Raffsberger's cat. How you responded to Jack's death. How you saved Zeus and cared for me. You're a good man with a generous heart and I love you. That still doesn't mean I'm not scared. One lawman cheated on me, yet, I think you're different."

"I am different," he whispered, pushing back a lock of hair that fell onto her face. "I love you, Taylor Braxton. I love you with my heart and soul, and I'm scared as well. There are some things I'm no longer willing to do. I'm not going to hide our relationship from anyone. I'm not sneaking around. You can have access to my phone, my emails, my Facebook account, all my personal information is at your disposal to make you feel secure that I'm not cheating on you."

He took her face in his hands, his mouth covering hers, kissing her with all the pain drifting away as he showed her how much she'd been missed.

Abruptly he broke the kiss. "There's one other thing..."

"What?" she said, staring at him as he stood.

He dropped down to one knee in front of her. "My other condition is that you marry me. I want to spend the rest of my life with you by my side. I want us to have a family and grow old together. I want to wake up each morning next to you. Will you please honor me and become my wife?"

She reached out and pulled him to her side, her eyes filling with tears. "Yes, I'll marry you. I love you, Ryan Jones. I love you so very much."

He wrapped his arms around her and held her tightly. "Promise me you won't tell our children about the Stupid Cupid

SYLVIA MCDANIEL

superstition. I don't want to arrest my children or have to take them home naked."

Laughing, she kissed his mouth. "No promises. I never believed in the superstition, but it brought us together. Love you."

"You too. Let's go home to that crazy dog of yours."

They stood and Taylor glanced at the statue.

"Thanks, Cupid," she said as she walked away, her arms wrapped tightly around her man.

Meghan's Story - Cupid Scores

MEGHAN'S HEART pounded within her chest, her breath coming out like frosted crystals in the night air as her bare feet slapped the pavement. Panic rose inside her and she promised herself a good cry when she reached safety.

She didn't know whether to circle back and try to find her purse and clothes or keep going. She was freezing as she ran butt naked down Main Street, glancing over her shoulder every few minutes.

"For someone with a Mensa IQ, you're not very smart," she scolded herself out loud.

Amazing how quickly you sobered up when faced with life and death consequences. If she didn't have frostbite from this little escapade, it would be a miracle. Her keys, her wallet, everything was in the park.

Her condo was a mile away. She had to keep moving toward her home and hope she could find the hidden spare key.

Headlights turned down the street and she dove behind shrubs, crouching, hiding, praying it wasn't the sheriff.

A red Corvette went screaming by and she rose from the bushes. Suddenly the car slammed on the brakes squealing the tires and she saw the back-up lights come on.

Crap, she'd been seen. She started running. Maybe if she just kept going, they would leave her alone.

The car pulled up alongside her and the window came down. She glanced over and her heart sank like the Titanic into the cold sea. Closing her eyes, she groaned. As if her luck couldn't get any worse tonight, Max Vandenberg smiled at her. "Darlin', it's a little chilly to be out streaking. You okay?"

"I'm perfectly fine," she retorted, continuing to run with her arms crossed over her breasts, her pride refusing to admit she needed help. Part of her wished he would go away. The rational, sane part of her screamed get in his car.

"Out for a midnight Cupid stroll," she said shivering.

He started laughing. "You did the Cupid dance. And if I was a betting man, I'd say the law showed up."

What could she say. The worst night of her life had just taken a turn into complete disaster. If that damn statue thought this was funny, she'd personally knock down the God of Love. She slowed from running to walking. It wasn't like Max hadn't seen her without clothes before.

"Get in the car," he said. "I'll take you home."

"What? Give up my midnight stroll?" She didn't want to crawl into that fancy car with her ex-high school boyfriend.

"Meghan, I know you're not stupid. And if anyone else comes along and sees the school librarian walking down the street naked, I think you'll be looking for a new profession. Get in the damn car."

The sound of a vehicle motor sent her fear soaring and she knew she had no choice. Jerking open the door of the Corvette, she hopped in the sports car.

"As much as I hate to cover up all those luscious curves, I think you need my coat. Don't want the cops seeing a naked woman in my car."

He handed her his jacket and she gladly slipped it on. The smell of Max wafted around her and memories of the two of them surged through her and she halted the memory tape before it reached the good parts.

He turned up the heater and she sighed with relief. Though she still hated Max, at this moment, he was a welcome sight. He put the car in drive and they pulled away just as the sheriff passed them going the other direction with Taylor in the backseat.

"Oh no, he caught Taylor," she said watching the car.

"Wow. Public indecency is not a charge you want on your record," he said.

Her chest ached for her friend. How could a night so full of fun turn so bad?

"Where did you leave your clothes?" he asked, watching the cop in his rearview mirror to make certain he continued down the road.

"My purse, my phone, my keys, my clothes, everything is on a bench in the city square," she said, knowing he would tease her about tonight's escapade.

He grinned. "You were doing the Cupid dance. Hey, if you're desperate for a boyfriend, I'm available."

Shaking her head, she grimaced, hating being in this position with him. "Been there, done that, and got the T-shirt along with a broken heart."

With a shrug, he smiled. "Second time around could be better than the first."

"Just take me home," she demanded, wondering why he would consider dating her again. He'd been the one who left for college hating her.

"Do you want me to go back and try to find your stuff?" he asked.

She wanted her things in a bad way, but she feared the sheriff would catch them. As the school librarian, she couldn't be caught.

"I don't think this car can be obscure. And I doubt the sheriff would leave my things in the park. But drive by and see if they're still there. I'll slump down in the seat," she said, thinking she was risking everything after getting away, but willing to gamble it all for the return of her purse.

The car's engine roared in the night as he turned it around in the middle of the street toward the park and that damn superstition that created this mess.

Slowly, he drove through the square and Meghan resisted flipping off the God of Love. She'd let herself be convinced to dance nude around a piece of rock that supposedly would find your true love. Land yourself in jail was more likely.

Instead, it had cost her dignity. Her reputation was on the line and possibly her job.

"Stupid statue," she muttered, trying to see her clothes as she peered out the window from the floor board. "They're gone."

With a sigh, she shook her head wondering if she needed to cancel her credit cards and phone, and have new locks installed on her condominium.

"What now? Do you have your keys to your condo?"

"If I can find the extra key without my neighbors calling the sheriff," she said.

"Where do you keep it?" he asked. "I'll find it while you wait in the car. Then I'll bring your robe out and you can put that on before you go into the house."

She frowned as she gazed at the man she'd loved passionately in high school. The man she'd given her virginity to and her heart until a costly mistake. "Why are you being so nice? You hate me."

He shrugged. "I'm a nice guy. I'm rescuing a damsel in distress."

Oh God. Now she would be beholding to him.

Punching the gas, he sped through the streets of town headed in the direction of her condo.

"How do you know where I live?" she asked.

He flashed that million-dollar smile the cameras loved. "Looked you up when I first moved back to Cupid. Wanted to make certain I didn't buy real estate in the same area as you."

"Ha! Like I could afford even a tenth of what you can."

"Probably not."

"So tell me the real reason you looked me up."

"Because I wanted to learn where you lived. So when I asked you out to dinner, I'd know where to pick you up. Only you keep saying no. After tonight, I think you owe me a date."

Meghan cursed. Yes, he'd asked her out several times at school, but she'd told him she had plans, she was busy. Anything to keep him from coming back into her life.

Now, everything she feared was happening all because of that damn statue in the square. And she owed him at least one date, but no more. While they were dating, he'd run when she needed him the most and she wasn't going to give him a second chance to show her he couldn't be counted on in a crisis. She was done with Max Vandenberg football super star.

For More Information on Cupid Scores check your favorite retailer!

Thank You For Reading!

Dear Reader,

Thanks for reading! I owe a big thank you to Krystal Shannan for inviting me into the Autism Box Set that is now no longer available. When I was trying to decide what book to write, I remembered that years ago, I wrote a story set in Cupid, Texas. I decided to go back to that little town and bring in new characters. I hope you enjoy the Cupid superstition.

As always, if you're inclined, please go to your favorite retailer and let others know what you think. Whether or not you loved the book or hated, it-I'd enjoy your feedback.

Sign up for my new book alerts if you'd like to learn about my releases before everyone else. Thanks for venturing into my world and I hope to see you here again soon.

Yours in Drama, Divas, Bad Boys and Romance!
Sincerely,

Sylvia McDaniel

www.SylviaMcDaniel.com
Sylvia@SylviaMcDaniel.com

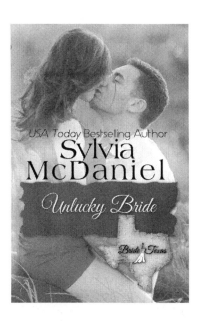

Chapter One

Cupid, Texas

"Laney Baxter, if you have reservations, back out now," Ally, her best friend and bridesmaid said. "Your son doesn't need a father that badly."

Reaching up, Laney touched the gold heart necklace around her neck. Maybe not, but the boy was growing from toddler to little boy, and her son would do better with the influence of a strong man.

Deliberately, she kept her son's father's identity a secret. No one needed to know, not her family, her friends, or even her best friend. For one thing, it would lead to all kinds of questions she was too embarrassed to explain. Especially to her parents.

"Not really reservations. Roger is just not who I envisioned marrying," Laney admitted, not willing to concede she dreamed of walking down the aisle with Ally's brother Chase.

"Do you love him? Please tell me you are not shackling yourself to a man you don't care about."

"Of course, I love Roger. He's a good man. But I expected I would be more excited about tomorrow," she confessed.

Roger was everything she could want. Patient and kind, he agreed to wait to consummate their relationship. After the pee stick changed color, she made the decision that until a ring graced her left finger and a license proclaimed her his wife, there would be no sharing her bed. What was that old saying?

Once burned, twice shy.

"Don't you think your lack of excitement is telling?"

Flipping her shoulder length brown hair back, she shook her head. "After being heartbroken by Trenton's dad, the disappearance of Jim, nothing about love excites me anymore. My lack of excitement is my attempt to guard my heart."

After an unplanned pregnancy and an abandoned engagement, when it came to men, caution was best.

Ally tossed back her glass of wine. "In high school, you were always the life of the party. Creating more mischief than any of the other girls we hung with. And yet, here you are the night before your big day holed up with me in The Cupid Love Nest bed and breakfast. Not even a bachelorette night on the town. We should be down at Valentino's bar drinking champagne and being toasted."

With a shrug, she said, "I'm a parent now. My son is my first priority."

The idea of getting drunk wasn't appealing. She only planned on marrying once and a clear head was optimal when she took her vows. What if Trenton became sick or called for her? He didn't need an out of control mother.

"Lord, I never realized how much having a child could change a person."

A laugh came from Laney's lips as she considered how her life had changed since Trenton arrived. At first, she'd been distraught over having a child. Now, Trenton was a blessing. When he grinned and held up his arms, her heart clenched with love for her little man. Forsaking her single lifestyle was easy.

Her only regret was his father.

Barely three years of age, Trenton's birth transformed her world for the better.

"Your mom is keeping him while you two go off on your honeymoon?"

"No honeymoon. We're spending the night in Fort Worth, and Sunday, we'll come back here. Monday, I move into his apartment," she said, thinking how odd it would be to leave her family home.

Living with them for twenty-four years was longer than she planned. After her parents learned of her pregnancy, they encouraged and helped her finish college while watching their grandson.

Because of their generosity, she had her bachelor's degree in elementary education. Leaving Trenton with her mother every day while she attended school, eased her mind that her son was looked after and so very loved.

Now, the time had come to grow up and face her responsibilities with a new husband.

Sipping the last of her bubbly, she thought back to that one night, when minus her panties, she let down her guard.

The superstition of dancing naked around the Cupid statue in the town square said the next person you met should be your true love. The consequences of her jaunt around that piece of rock appeared nine months later with the delivery of her beautiful baby boy.

Shame, his father didn't have the courage to listen to her when she tried to tell him the results of their one night together where even a condom didn't stop her from getting pregnant. Instead, he'd been too busy going off to graduate school than to learn they were expecting.

One day when Trenton was old enough, they would have a long talk about his father. It would be hard to keep the bitterness from her voice and the anger from her words. His father followed his dreams while she had their child.

"If you decide against this wedding, you're welcome to escape to the family cabin on the banks of the Leon River right outside Bride, Texas. That crazy little town started by the jilted bride."

"A jilted bride started that hole in the wall?"

"Yes, she was stood up by her fiancé and she created a life for herself right there. A beautiful story to remind brides that sometimes there is something better coming along," Ally said, smiling. "It's one of the reasons I like it there."

"Thank you, but I won't need a place. I'm getting married in twenty-four hours."

"Well, here's the key to the cabin," Ally said, dangling the metal like a temptation. "I'll carry it in my bouquet, just in case."

Laney giggled. "Thanks, but next week, I'll be moving into Roger's apartment as his wife and he as Trenton's father."

Ally took a deep sigh and released it. "You realize you have the worst luck with guys. What makes you think marriage will be any better?"

"Yes, I agree I'm unlucky when it comes to men," she said, her eyes blinking with unshed tears.

This was her second endeavor at standing before a preacher and saying vows. Not long after the birth of Trenton, she met Jim who asked her to marry him, only six weeks before the ceremony, he walked away. Disappeared without a call, without a trace.

An unplanned pregnancy, a broken engagement, and now the night before her big day, she had jitters. Nothing more than nerves.

Ally shook her head. "Don't know why, I always thought you would wed Chase. Ever since my brother picked you up that night we dared you to dance in the buff around Cupid, I pictured the two of you together."

"Sometimes even Cupid gets it wrong," she said, knowing she thought she would wed him as well.

ó.

Laney stood in the vestibule of the church, in her white satin dress and veil waiting for the wedding march to begin. Doubts assailed her like hail in a Texas thunderstorm. Just like Ally had the night before, she questioned if she should marry Roger.

A gorgeous, rock-solid man who had a great job, supported her, treated her special, kissed well...*but not as earth moving like the man who broke your heart,* her conscious reminded her.

Reaching up, she touched the gold heart necklace, still wondering who had sent her the jewelry. Not long after she did the Cupid dance, it arrived in an unmarked box. No return address, no name, nothing. Now, she considered it her lucky charm.

"Are you certain?" her father asked. "It's not too late to back out."

"Let's go, Daddy," she said, refusing to let her apprehension overcome her. "He's a good man."

"Yes, he is," her father replied. "Is he the right man for my daughter?"

"Come on, Dad. They're waiting," she said, plastering a smile on her face, not answering. That would be a long discussion. One they didn't have time for.

"Okay, let's go," he said and patted her on the hand.

Walking down the aisle, she barely glanced at the people who were seated. Her eyes were on the man she was about to commit her life to, hoping she was making the right choice.

As she neared Roger, she noticed he appeared anxious. Sweat

beaded on his forehead. Of course, he was nervous. They were making a lifetime commitment today. A major life event.

Smiling, she tried to reassure him as she approached the altar.

"Who gives this woman away?"

"Her mother and I," her father said, handing her off to Roger. Placing her hand in his, she gave a quick, reassuring squeeze.

The pastor looked out at the people gathered for the ceremony. "Should there be anyone who has cause why this couple should not be united in holy matrimony, please say so now."

The door of the church slammed open and the sound of high-heels running down the aisle had her frowning as she watched Roger's eyes widened, his mouth dropped open, and she knew. Like a bolt of lightning, she just knew...

The color faded from her fiancé's face as he gasped, and her stomach tightened. Taking a deep breath, she fortified herself for the bad news. Unlucky again.

"Excuse me, but this man is married," a shrill voice sounded as their friends and family mumbled to each other.

A short woman with bottled-blonde hair and a set of decorated designer boobs displayed down to the top of her nipples, stood waving a piece of paper, a hefty rock on her left hand. "This is a copy of the marriage license. I have a ring on my finger and our wedding photo."

Reaching for her beacon of hope, Laney's fingers flew to the golden heart necklace around her throat.

Relief seemed to flood Laney and the look of horror on Roger's face made her burst out laughing. From the distress etched on his face, she grasped the woman's claim was true. Anger flooded her body like a Texas downpour racing through the streets. The man who supposedly loved her let her make a complete fool of herself.

"You low-life jerk," she said low enough for only his ears. "You're married. When were you going to tell me?"

"No, no," he cried as she walked back down the petal covered carpet, her satin skirt swishing, determination in every step to elude this fiasco.

"The marriage is not real. It happened in Vegas," Roger howled. "Stop, Laney, stop."

"Oh, yes, it did," the woman said. "We met, spent the night together, and woke up the next morning in wedded bliss. After I went to get coffee, you left before we talked about where we're going to live."

"That was fake," he exclaimed.

"Oh no, baby. This sealed document is as real as it gets. You belong to me."

Nearing the heavily made-up woman, Laney sensed her parents surrounding her, her precious son in her mother's arms. The touch of her father's hand at her elbow, guiding her around the circus she could see unfolding there in the church, was comforting.

Roger begged his new wife to stop as she shoved the paper that shackled him to the platinum bombshell in his face. "Honey, I'm so glad I showed up. Bigamy is against the law."

"Right now, jail would be better than the hell I'm living."

The vulgar woman laughed. "That's not what you said in bed the other night."

Hurrying past the unfolding chaos, a loud scuffling noise came from behind. Looking over her shoulder to see Roger sprawled in the aisle, a satisfied look of retaliation spread on her grandmother's face.

Granny could be deadly with her cane, buying Laney time to escape the auditorium. Smiling at the woman she loved, she gave her a thumbs up.

Laney hurried out the chapel. Funny, she wasn't crying. She wasn't even sad. Actually, she felt at peace. As they reached the vestibule, she turned to her mother and took her son from her arms.

"What are you doing?" her mother asked, emerald eyes filled with tears.

"I'm leaving town for a little while," she said, knowing instinctively this was what she should do. Hide out from the drama swirling around her and Roger. Getting away was the only reason she would have any serenity. Moving as swift as her taffeta skirt would allow, she made her way past the stunned wedding planner.

"Let me keep Trenton," her mother said, running after her.

"Thank you, Mom, but I need my son. Give me a chance to get away, and I promise, I'll call you later. At the moment, I must leave."

The impulse to race as fast as she could from the scene of her latest disaster sped through her like the adrenaline of running. The fight or flight urge was all flight. The flaxen-haired sex kitten could have Roger.

In a fog, she entered the bride's room, picked up the overnight bag. Trenton would need more clothes in a few days or a washing machine would work, but she didn't care. Thank goodness, her suitcase was already in the trunk of her car.

Soon as she could grab the rest of her stuff, she would run out the building, though she had no plan where she would go.

Following behind her into the suite, her mother's face was streaked with tears. A distressed frown crinkled her father's forehead as he tried to comfort her mother while he scrutinized his daughter.

"Mom, I'm all right. Let me slip away so Roger can't reach me. The wedding was ruined by his lovely new wife and I hope they're very unhappy together."

"Your mother stopped me from punching him," her father said. "I wanted to deck him."

"Thank you," she said, her heart aching for the hurt her parents were feeling as she reached over and kissed them each on the cheek. Just then, she heard Roger's voice yelling for her at the top of his lungs.

"Mom, Dad, I'm sorry, I've got to get out of here. Trust me, I'm okay, but I don't want to speak to him."

Reaching into his pocket, her father pulled out a wad of cash. "In case you need something. Don't forget to call. We'll be waiting to hear from you."

"As soon as we arrive," she said and squeezed her mother's arm.

"Be careful," her mother said and her father wrapped her in his arms.

Picking up her bags, Laney rushed down the hall to the chapel exit, her wedding dress swishing. If only she had time to change clothes. At the door, she saw Ally leaning against the frame, twirling a key.

"Told you so," she said and handed her the shining metal.

"I don't..." The cabin was the perfect place. A small little house tucked on the river, away from town, away from everyone until the melodramatics died down. The kind of place to disappear for a while. Soak up the sun and rest.

"The weather is supposed to become nasty later today, so be watchful. Call me if you have any trouble," Ally said. "Even if you want a little company."

Laney gave her an awkward hug. "This is why I love you. Trenton and I will enjoy the solitude and the quiet."

When the dust settled, she would tell Ally how right she was about her luck with men, but right now, she had to leave or face Roger.

"Now, go. Somehow a reporter showed up and is wanting to do a story on the Unlucky Bride. An interview you don't want to give."

A sarcastic laugh bubbled up from within her. "Why do I have the worst luck when it comes to men?" A glance at her son and her heart swelled with love. "Except that one time I got you, buddy."

"Go," Ally commanded. "And be careful of the—"

Suddenly a flash bulb went off in her face. Ducking her son's head, she ran to her car - all decorated with streamers announcing they were man and wife.

A curse slipped from her lips.

"No, Mommy, bad word," Trenton told her.

"You're right, son. Mommy won't say it again," she promised.

"Where's Roger?" he asked.

"Gone for good," she said and buckled him in his seat.

Starting the car, she drove out of the parking lot, prophylactics flying from her grill, tin cans bouncing behind her, streamers proclaiming just married. More like, publicly dumped.

❧

Thunder rumbled, the house shuddering as Chase Hamilton stared out the window at the rain streaming from the sky. Why in the hell had he come here to this little cabin in the middle of godforsaken nowhere?

Growing up in Cupid, Texas, where people danced naked around a boy in a diaper sculpture to find their true love, he was shocked to learn how a jilted woman started this beautiful community. His parents' weekend getaway sat about a hundred feet from the Leon River, right outside Bride, Texas - where jilted women sought answers to their love life.

What about cheated on men? Where did they go?

To a home along the Leon River to heal. Two broken ribs, a black eye, and a bruised heart. In an irresponsible act of rage, he threw the first punch, creating a scene and barely escaping arrest. All because Cissy, who he enjoyed dating, didn't believe in monogamy. Now, he asked himself, had she been worth all the pain and anger.

Hell, no.

Limping away from the window, he sank back onto the couch, placing the ice pack on his bruised body. Staring at the blank screen of the television, he pondered his life, taking stock of where to go from here.

"Fighting is for losers," he said out loud, his brain agreeing with him. His heart saying *come on, you'd punch the jerk again.*

You don't hit women, children, or animals and the man had done two out of three in front of Chase causing him to lose his meager self-control.

Sadly, Cissy's dramatics outweighed the positives and left him reeling. In the end, she'd chosen the muscled brute over Chase, regardless that the wrestler kicked her dog and slapped her beautiful face.

That kind of crazy, he didn't need - though until then, she seemed so perfect.

Headlights flashed through the darkened room and slowly he rose to his feet. Who could be driving out here in this awful weather? No one knew he had escaped here to lick his wounds and mend in private.

A small Honda splashed on the dirt drive leading to the house. What were they doing coming out here now?

The car stopped and a woman opened the car door and stepped out. Her head bent to avoid the slashing rain drops as she reached inside the backseat of the car. As the woman turned and faced him, his chest tightened, his stomach churned, and he couldn't believe his eyes.

Laney Baxter in a long, lace wedding dress dashed through the puddles running toward the cabin, a little boy in her arms. The memory of their one night together slammed into his gut, wrenching his very soul and he groaned. Not what his recovery needed.

Stepping under the awning, she set the child down and he

heard the key in the lock. Chase yanked the door open and she jumped back, her eyes wide with fright.

"Chase," she said in shock, her emerald eyes widening. How he loved gazing into her eyes, feeling like he'd come home.

Shaking his head, he confirmed his eyes weren't betraying him, she was indeed wearing a wedding gown.

"Where's the groom?"

"Left him at church," she said, emptying water out of her shoes.

"What the hell are you doing here? Where did you get a key?"

"Ally told me I could use the cabin for a while."

"Well, she's wrong. You've got to leave."

Laney reached up and ran her hand through her wet hair and glanced down at her son who stared up at her in confusion. "Momma?"

"Ally didn't tell me you would be here. I'm sorry," she said. "I thought I would be alone."

"She doesn't know I'm here. No one knows and I want to keep it that way."

"Little late for that," she said. "When I return, she's going to want to know why."

The little boy tugged on the tulle of her gown and Chase wondered what happened that she came here and not on her fabulous honeymoon.

"Momma," he said a little louder.

How could a man or a woman hit a child or an animal? Yes, he'd been wrong to stoop to the man's level, and yes, he was paying the price for his rage. When his fist connected with the tough wrestler's cheek, the explosion of flesh and bone felt good, until his retaliation shot landed in Chase's ribs.

Never one to wrestle and throw a punch quickly, he had been no match against the professional.

Glancing down at the child, the vision of a screaming toddler invading his personal space made his decision. They had to leave.

"Tell her you couldn't reach the house. Tell her anything. But you can't stay here."

"You're going to send us back out into the storm," she said, her eyes narrowing.

The two of them shared one magical night of being together, and right now, his heart was dealing with his latest love disaster leaving him vulnerable. Too vulnerable to the charms of Laney. Even in her wet, muddied, now ruined, wedding dress, her mahogany hair falling around her shoulders, she looked stunning.

Whatever happened, the man had been a fool to let her go, and Chase couldn't be around her. Not now, not even with a downpour raging outside. She was hurricane force winds of danger compared to cold front Cissy.

"Momma, I need to go potty," the little boy said impatiently. "Now."

"Can my son at least use your restroom before we go back out into the storm?"

A twinge of guilt gripped him and his logical side reminded him of the dangers.

"Of course," he said. He wasn't a complete monster. Just a man confused and hurt and trying to recover.

Taking the boy by the hand, she led him into the living area and straight to the bathroom. In fewer than five minutes, they returned.

"Come on, son, let's go."

"We're not staying?"

"No, we're not," she said defiantly and walked out the door without saying goodbye. "Men are such dicks."

Peering out at the pouring rain, he watched from the door as she loaded the little boy into the child seat in the back of the car. Regret ate at his insides, he should stop her. The thought of a kid running through the house, making noise and the constant presence of Laney kept his lips shut.

Climbing into the car, she started the vehicle and backed away.

Chase closed the door, the silence eating at him. He should have let her stay. Frustrated, but thinking he'd been heartless, he yanked open the door to stop her. Running into the rain after her, to keep her from going, all he saw were tail lights going down the long drive.

One minute, he was trying to save someone and getting injured in the process, and the next, he was sending a woman and child out in a storm. Maybe she was right. Maybe he was just as much of a dick as Cissy's new love.

To Continue Reading Go to Your Favorite Retailer!

A Sneak Peek at The Wanted Bride!

"I need a one-way ticket to anywhere," Valerie Burrows commanded the girl behind the bus counter in downtown Dallas. A charred piece of her wedding veil sagged onto her face. Impatiently, she flipped the singed lace away, her throat closing off the tears that threatened her vision.

On what was supposed to be the happiest day of her life, she reeked of smoke, not flowers, saw red not white, tasted bile not cake.

Glancing up from the counter the clerk's eyes widened, making Valerie acutely aware of her appearance. On what was supposed to be the happiest day of her life, she felt traumatized, not joyous.

"Whe...re do you want to go?" the clerk stammered.

"Anywhere, as long as I leave in the next five minutes," Valerie insisted, wishing people would stop staring. So she looked like a crazy woman. After this morning maybe she was a little loco.

"The bus to Amarillo is loading now," the agent advised, her large brown eyes riveted to Valerie. "I have one seat left. The one-way fare is sixty-five dollars."

Though she preferred to travel by plane, there was no time or way to get to the airport. She could take the bus or stay and face the consequences of her actions.

Valerie dug the cash out of her Bottega Veneta purse and handed the money to the ticket agent. "I'll take it."

Dirty lace from her wedding veil fell onto her face again, so she yanked the offending garment off her head and threw the veil on top of her matching Louis Vuitton luggage.

The beautiful lace of her Vera Wang wedding gown was streaked with gray and black. Burn streaks made a crazy pattern on the silk that didn't accessorize the seed pearls.

The heel of one of her Stuart Weitzman pumps had snapped several blocks ago, and her feet were blistered. And yet her heart beat on in spite of her ruined wedding.

The clerk handed her the ticket, sympathy in her dark eyes. "The bus is ready. You're the last one to board."

Not even time to change. Head held high, spine locked in place, she limped to the white steel carriage, her suitcases trailing behind.

There, she handed her two suitcases to a gawking young man. He opened his mouth. "Just load my luggage."

She glanced up to see faces pressed against the glass windows of the bus, gaping at her like she was a freak show.

Hadn't these people ever seen a runaway bride in real life before? Julia Roberts may have made the movie, but she didn't own the copyright to wedding disasters.

With her carry-on bag hanging from her shoulder, Valerie marched up the steps of the waiting bus as if she walked around in a wedding gown every day. The babble of sixty voices ceased as she handed the driver her ticket.

Her silk dress pressed against her legs and swished as she made her way to the only empty seat on her getaway bus. Thank God she'd ditched the petticoats in the Corvette.

A gray-haired woman glanced at her as she put her luggage in the overhead bin.

"Hm hm hm, I can't wait to hear this story," the elderly Hispanic woman said. "Are you all right?"

Valerie plopped in the seat, her ruined silk gown making a mighty swish. She exhaled loudly, her heart aching, her eyes blurring with unshed tears. For the last hour she'd been holding her breath while making her escape.

But now, now all the pain she'd carefully controlled broke free and she chuckled. Hysterical laughter rumbled from deep inside her, echoed through the bus. A single tear rolled down her cheek. "I am now."

For More Information Check Your Favorite Retailer!

Also By Sylvia McDaniel

Return to Cupid, Texas
Cupid Stupid
Cupid Scores
Cupid's Dance
Cupid Help Me!
Cupid Cures
Cupid's Heart
Cupid Santa
Cupid Second Chance
Return to Cupid Box Set Books 1-3

Contemporary Romance
My Sister's Boyfriend
The Wanted Bride
The Reluctant Santa
The Relationship Coach
Secrets, Lies, & Online Dating

Bride, Texas Multi-Author Series
The Unlucky Bride

The Langley Legacy
Collin's Challenge

Short Sexy Reads
Racy Reunions Series
Paying For the Past
Her Christmas Lie
Cupid's Revenge

Science/Fiction Paranormal

The Magic Mirror Series
Touch of Decadence
Touch of Deceit

Western Historicals
A Hero's Heart
Ace's Bride
Second Chance Cowboy
Ethan

American Brides
Katie: Bride of Virginia

The Burnett Brides Series
The Rancher Takes A Bride
The Outlaw Takes A Bride
The Marshal Takes A Bride
The Christmas Bride
Boxed Set

Lipstick and Lead Series
Desperate
Deadly
Dangerous
Daring
Determined
Deceived

Scandalous Suffragettes of the West
Abigail
Bella
Callie – Coming Soon
Faith
Mistletoe Scandal

Southern Historical Romance
A Scarlet Bride

The Cuvier Women
Wronged
Betrayed
Beguiled
Boxed Set

Receive a free book when you sign up for my new book alerts!

USA TODAY Best Selling Author, Sylvia McDaniel has published over forty western historical and contemporary romance novels. Known for her sweet, funny, family-oriented romances, Sylvia is the author of The Burnett Brides a historical western series, The Cuvier Widows, a Louisiana historical series, Lipstick and Lead, a western historical series and several short contemporary romances.

Former President of the Dallas Area Romance Authors, a member of the Romance Writers of America®, and a member of Novelists Inc, her novel, A Hero's Heart was a 1996 Golden Heart Finalist. Several other books have placed or won in the San Antonio Romance Authors Contest, LERA Contest, and she was a Golden Network Finalist.

Married for over twenty years to her best friend, they have two dachshunds and a good-looking, grown son who thinks there's no place like home. She loves gardening, hiking, shopping, knitting and football (Cowboys and Bronco's fan).

www.SylviaMcDaniel.com
The End!

Made in the USA
Monee, IL
27 April 2021